'Shh,' said Mandy, cocking her head on one side. 'Listen.'

Thump, thump.

Mandy scrambled out of her sleeping bag and pulled on her trainers and fleece. 'I think it's coming from the *Halcyon*,' she said. 'We'd better go and find out.'

They crept out of the tent and stood for a moment in the dark night, listening. The moon shone brightly through the branches of the willow trees, casting shadows on the ground.

'It's Bob!' Mandy cried in amazement.

The rabbit was thumping insistently on the wooden deck of the *Halcyon*, his ears flat against his back and his whole body trembling.

'What is it, Bob?' Mandy asked in concern, climbing aboard. 'Is it Stanley?' She suddenly remembered that rabbits thumped their back legs when they sensed danger. A cold feeling of fear crept into her heart.

Animal Ark series

Plus:

Little Animal Ark
Animal Ark Pets
Animal Ark Hauntings
Animal Ark Holiday Specials

LUCY DANIELS

Bunny
— on a —
Barge

Illustrations by Ann Baum

Hodder
Children's
Books

a division of Hodder Headline Limited

Special thanks to Lucy Courtenay

Thanks also to C. J. Hall, B.Vet.Med., M.R.C.V.S., for reviewing the veterinary information contained in this book.

First published in Great Britain in 2002
by Hodder Children's Books

For more information about Animal Ark,
please contact www.animalark.co.uk

10 9 8 7 6 5 4 3 2 1

A Catalogue record for this book is available from the British
Library

ISBN 0 340 85112 0

Typeset by Avon Dataset Ltd, Bidford-on-Avon, Warks

Printed and bound in Great Britain by
Clays Ltd, St Ives plc

Hodder Children's Books
a division of Hodder Headline Limited
338 Euston Road
London NW1 3BH

One

'James, look! A kingfisher!' Mandy Hope called as a turquoise flash of feathers flew past and disappeared into the reeds. 'Did you see it?' she asked.

James Hunter shook his head and took off his glasses, polishing them on the hem of his T-shirt. 'Where did it come from?'

Mandy pointed up the river. 'Over there, I think,' she said. 'Its nest must be on the riverbank somewhere. I've never seen a kingfisher before, but those blue feathers were a real giveaway!'

'You were lucky,' said James, putting his glasses

back on. 'They aren't very common.' He flopped down on a sunny patch of grass. 'I wouldn't mind living on a riverbank,' he said, smiling. 'It would be like camping for ever.'

'Till you got hungry, you mean!' Mandy teased, pushing back her dark blonde hair and sitting down next to her friend.

Together, they stared out at the shining river. They were a couple of miles downstream from Mandy and James's home village of Welford. Barges and motorboats lined the water's edge. A breeze ruffled the river's unbroken surface, and a couple of ducks quacked lazily on the far side of the water.

As Mandy and James lay in the sun, James's labrador, Blackie, tore out of the undergrowth, his ears pricked. They watched him zig-zagging from left to right, sniffing the grass. He lifted his glossy black head and barked before disappearing into the long grass again.

'Blackie's full of energy today, isn't he?' Mandy commented.

'He can tell it's the first day of the holidays,' James answered. 'I know how he feels!'

Mandy grinned, immediately getting to her feet. 'OK, then, race you down the path!'

'Hey!' James protested, scrambling up. 'That's cheating!'

Mandy flew down the towpath with James close behind. Blackie shot ahead. All three of them ran, Blackie barking madly, until they reached a bend in the river. There, they came to a stop beside a barge, laughing and catching their breath. Blackie started running round in circles, faster and faster, barking with excitement.

'All right, all right, Blackie!' said James breathlessly. 'Calm down!'

There was a loud crash as the cabin door of the nearby barge flew open. Mandy and James jumped and turned round in surprise. A white-haired old man with a furious scowl was standing on the deck of the barge. Blackie stopped barking and stood still, his tail wagging uncertainly.

The old man folded his arms and glared down at Mandy and James. He was tall and lean, his clothes faded by the sun. 'Control that dog of yours!' he growled. 'Or I'll have something to say about it to the river police!'

'We're very—' Mandy began.

'Clear off, the pair of you!' the old man cut in sharply. With a final glare, he disappeared back inside, slamming the cabin door behind him.

'Oops,' said Mandy, after a short silence.

James frowned. 'He seemed pretty cross, didn't he? Blackie wasn't making *that* much noise.'

Mandy looked at Blackie, who was lying down now, his face tucked between his front paws. 'I suppose that any noise is too much noise for some people,' she said with a sigh. She checked her watch. 'It's probably time to head home, anyway.'

They started walking along the riverbank, back towards Welford. Blackie trotted ahead quietly. Mandy looked back over her shoulder at the barge. It was painted in vibrant shades of turquoise, orange and white, with the name *Halcyon* written across its bow in silver paint. Someone had painted a small kingfisher flashing along the side of the cabin, wings whirring and a silvery fish clasped in its beak. A small boat with an outboard motor bobbed beside it, attached to the barge by a length of orange rope.

Suddenly there was a strange rustling sound in the undergrowth.

'Look!' Mandy gasped, grabbing James by the arm.

'What?' said James, surprised. 'Look at what?'

'There!' Mandy insisted, pointing.

A flash of something black appeared for a split second in the grass. Then it vanished.

'Blackie?' Mandy called uncertainly. 'Is that you?'

Hearing his name, Blackie bounded back along the path towards Mandy and James. Suddenly he pressed his nose to the ground, whining with excitement, his tail a frantic blur.

'Blackie's smelled it, whatever it was,' said James.

Mandy squatted down and peered into the grass.

'There!' James gave a shout.

Mandy spun round, just in time to see a large black and white rabbit disappearing into the grass further down the path. Blackie gave a yelp of surprise, and tore off in hot pursuit.

'What's a tame-looking rabbit doing out here?' Mandy gasped in astonishment.

'Blackie, come back!' called James. '*Blackie*!'

Blackie ignored him, snuffling madly in all directions as the rabbit vanished.

Mandy squinted along the path. 'It must have escaped from somewhere,' she frowned, worried. 'Blackie, come *here!*'

Blackie gave up his hunt, and trotted slowly back towards Mandy and James.

James clipped Blackie's lead on to his collar. 'At least the rabbit's safe from you now.' He grinned down at the dog, patting him on his smooth, warm head.

'Not that it was ever in any danger from Blackie!' Mandy laughed. 'Come on, let's see if we can find it.'

They hunted along both sides of the path, as hard as they could. But there was no sign of it. At last James straightened up with a sigh, pushing his brown hair out of his eyes. 'It's not here,' he said. 'Maybe it lives on one of the barges.'

'Hmmm, maybe,' said Mandy. She looked up and down the river. There were several colourful boats moored at the edge, bobbing gently in the water. James was probably right. The rabbit must belong to one of the barges.

James looked at his watch. 'We ought to head back,' he said. He tugged at Blackie's lead to bring the dog to heel. Walking in single file, he and Mandy slowly followed the path back home.

* * *

It was a lovely walk back to Welford, along the towpath in the dappled shade of willows and beech trees. The river narrowed about a kilometre from the village. The route narrowed too, turning from a smooth, grassy path to a pebbly little track. Mandy and James crossed the wooden footbridge to walk the last few hundred yards up to the village.

'Still thinking about that rabbit?' asked James.

'Yes,' Mandy admitted with a frown. 'Maybe it does belong to someone on the boats, but it was still strange, seeing it on the path like that. It looked like a family pet, didn't it?'

'I've never seen a wild rabbit that's black and white,' James agreed.

Blackie had already reached the Fox and Goose pub, and was waiting patiently for Mandy and James at the turning for Animal Ark, where Mandy lived. Mandy's parents were vets, and their surgery was attached to their old stone cottage.

'Let's go and find Mum,' Mandy suggested. 'She'll probably be in the surgery. We can tell her about the rabbit.'

Jean Knox, the Animal Ark receptionist, looked up as Mandy and James came into the cool, airy waiting room. 'You look hot,' she said. 'Nice walk?'

'Lovely,' smiled Mandy, dropping down into one of the waiting room chairs. 'We saw a kingfisher. And—'

She was interrupted by the phone. It was always difficult having more than a short conversation during the surgery's opening hours.

'That's nice,' said Jean, hunting around the desk for the appointments book. 'Your parents are in the kitchen by the way, Mandy. They've got an interesting visitor with them,' she added, one hand hovering over the ringing phone. 'I think she might like to hear about the kingfisher.' She smiled at them, and then picked up the receiver. 'Good afternoon, Animal Ark.'

Mandy and James walked into the bright, cheery kitchen. Blackie padded after them and flopped down on to the cool kitchen floor.

Emily Hope, Mandy's mother, was sitting at the table, deep in conversation with someone who had their back to the door. Adam Hope was standing by the fridge, pouring iced fruit juice into three glasses.

'Hello, you two,' said Mandy's mum. 'Look who's dropped in to see us.'

The visitor turned round and smiled.

Mandy grinned at the visitor with delight. 'Hi, Michelle! Have you got some more research for us?'

Michelle Holmes's TV programme *Wildlife Ways* was one of Mandy's favourite shows. Mandy and James had helped Michelle with some wildlife research in the past, and Michelle often came to them for help with her new projects.

'You two are keen!' said Mr Hope with a grin. He poured two more glasses of juice for Mandy and James, put all the glasses on the table and sat down beside Mandy's mum. 'School's only just broken up and already you want more work?'

'It's good to see you and James again,' said Michelle warmly. 'I've just been talking to your parents about our new programme, and I might have a job or two for you.' She took a sip of her fruit juice.

Mandy sat down at the kitchen table. 'What's the project this time?' she asked.

Michelle placed her glass carefully on the table, her eyes sparkling. 'We're going to be doing a six-part programme on and around the river,' she told them. 'There should be lots of animal activity at this time of year. We thought we'd focus under the water as well as on the bank, so we see life from both sides. The producer thinks it's a great idea, and can't wait to get started. We're just starting to map out the programmes and gather as much information as we can about nesting sites, river habitats, spawning grounds for fish – that kind of thing.'

'We've just come from the river,' said James. 'Mandy saw a kingfisher.'

'A kingfisher? Well done!' exclaimed Michelle, turning to Mandy.

'I only saw it for a moment,' Mandy admitted. 'But it was beautiful. Such an amazing blue!'

'Kingfishers are so fast, I'm surprised if anyone ever sees them for longer than a split second,' said Michelle, scribbling something down on a pad of paper. 'Where did you see it? Do you think you could show me some time?'

Mandy nodded enthusiastically. 'Sure, whenever you like.' She took a quick sip of her drink. 'But I'll tell you what else we saw,' she said in a more serious voice. 'A rabbit. It was just hopping along the path.'

'Sounds quite normal to me. What did you

expect it to do?' said Mr Hope, surprised.

Mandy rolled her eyes. 'Not a wild rabbit, Dad! A tame one. A black and white pet rabbit. We think it must belong to one of the people who live on the barges. It certainly looked like it knew where it was going.'

'Did you try and catch it?' asked Mr Hope.

'Blackie tried!' said James. 'But it disappeared.'

'You're probably right about it belonging to one of the barges,' said Emily Hope. 'People do sometimes let domestic rabbits roam about freely in their house and garden. But I can't say I've ever heard of a rabbit that lived on a boat before! Keep an eye out for it next time you're down there, won't you? Just in case it has escaped from someone's house.'

Michelle was looking thoughtful. 'It would be nice if we could get some human interest in the programme,' she said. 'After all, people live on the river as well!' She looked at Mandy and James. 'We could really use some help with finding where to film, good hiding places for the cameras – places that are within sight of the wildlife. How well do you know the river?'

'Pretty well,' Mandy said. 'We know where the

moorhens have been nesting recently, and where the herons like to fish.'

'I think there are water voles, too,' put in James. 'They often leave droppings in the grass between the path and the river. We haven't seen any actual voles yet, but we know more or less where to look.'

'Exactly what we need.' Michelle smiled. 'Did you know that voles are an endangered species these days?'

Mandy nodded. 'Rivers are becoming so polluted that the voles are dying out,' she said sadly.

'So you think you could help us find our way around?'

'Definitely!' said Mandy. 'Just say the word.'

'Then that's settled,' said Michelle, getting up and straightening her light cotton trousers. 'How about tomorrow morning?'

Mandy and James grinned at each other. Tomorrow morning would be perfect!

Two

As Mandy dashed around Animal Ark, getting ready, Mrs Hope was ticking things off on her fingers.

'Sun cream?'

'Got it,' Mandy puffed, bounding up the stairs two at a time.

'Water?'

'Got it,' Mandy called down the stairs.

'Money?'

Mandy grabbed a sunhat from her dressing table. She rushed back to the landing and took the stairs in four flying leaps, landing with a thump in front of her mum. 'Got it.'

'Right, James should be here at any moment,' said Emily Hope. 'And Michelle's due in about ten minutes. OK?'

'OK!' Mandy grinned. On cue, the doorbell rang. 'See you!' she called, stepping outside.

James was standing on the steps, adjusting the straps of his rucksack.

'Hi,' Mandy said breathlessly. 'Michelle's not here yet, but she should turn up any minute. Where's Blackie?' she added in surprise, glancing around the sunny driveway.

'I left him at home,' said James, heaving his rucksack back on to his shoulders. 'I thought he might frighten away any wildlife.'

They sat together on the steps of the surgery, waiting for Michelle to arrive. Soon they heard the crunch of tyres on the drive, and a dark green car swung round and pulled to a stop.

Michelle wound down the window. 'All set?'

Mrs Hope came outside, buttoning her white coat and checking her watch. 'It's going to be hot again today, so make sure you drink plenty of water,' she said.

'Busy day ahead, Emily?' asked Michelle.

Mrs Hope nodded. 'As ever! Some of us aren't lucky enough to get outside for more than a quick cup of tea!' She smiled. 'Hope you see the kingfisher again.'

The car pulled away through the village and on to the road that ran parallel to the river. Mandy stared out of the window, watching the river twinkling beside them as the car rushed along.

'I'd just like to check out a few places and make some preliminary notes today,' said Michelle over her shoulder. 'I'd love to find that kingfisher, so stay on the lookout.'

'Definitely,' Mandy promised. 'And there's a spot on the weir where the herons like to fish. You can't miss the moorhens' nest either – it's right in the middle of the river. We'll look out for water voles too.' She crossed her fingers tightly. It would be wonderful to see one of those beautiful, shy creatures.

The riverside car park was almost empty as they drove in. It was still only 8.30, but already the sun felt hot on their faces. Stepping out of the car, Mandy looked around. She could see the path she and James had walked along yesterday, following the river back in the direction of Welford.

Michelle stood beside Mandy and looked up the river, shielding her eyes from the glare of the sun. 'So where did the kingfisher come from?' she asked.

Mandy frowned. 'It came from upstream, and flew into some reeds over there.'

'Right, let's see what we can find!' said Michelle, grabbing her rucksack.

They made their way up the river until they reached the reed bed Mandy had pointed out. The reeds grew in a small shady inlet. Ducking under some overhanging willow branches, Mandy and James hunted for signs of a kingfisher's nest in the bank. But they saw nothing except for a couple of white-headed coots and, close to the water's edge, a pair of trout flicking their tails against the current.

There was a tiny plop to their right. Mandy spun round – just in time to see something small and dark brown slipping off a mound of weed into the river. 'A water vole!' she gasped. She couldn't believe her luck. 'I just caught a glimpse of its tail.'

'Wow!' said James, almost dropping his glasses in his excitement.

Michelle scribbled something in her notebook. 'Wonderful!' she smiled. 'Since the kingfisher is nowhere to be seen, I wonder if we'll be able to find the voles' nest instead?'

Mandy and James threw themselves enthusiastically into the task of locating the nest. They lay down on the river's edge in turns, peering left and right along the wet, muddy riverbank.

'This is a time when we could really use some kind of mirror,' sighed Mandy, as she wriggled out over the water as far as she dared to examine a small hole close to the waterline. 'If I hang any further over the edge, I'm going to end up falling in.'

She peered more closely at a small, neat hole in the bank. The mouth of the hole was worn smooth, as if something was going in and out of it regularly. Could it be a nest? Holding her breath, Mandy watched the opening for any sign of movement.

Suddenly the roar of a motorboat shattered the morning peace. Mandy and James looked up to see a shining white prow carving a fast, deep line through the water as it raced downriver. It swerved mid-stream, slowing down to a gradual halt.

'Look out!' James shouted, scrambling backwards as fast as he could. But it was too late. The wake of the boat washed over the edge of the riverbank, soaking Mandy to the skin. Water flew around James's feet, soaking his trainers.

'Urgh!' Mandy spluttered, shaking her head and pulling herself clear of the bank.

James glared indignantly at the boat, which was now pulling in to moor on the far side of the river, slightly further downstream. He coughed at the boat's clouds of dirty exhaust.

Mandy brushed herself off and shook the water from her blonde hair.

Michelle Holmes rushed over. 'Are you two OK?'

'Yes,' Mandy said ruefully, looking down at her soggy T-shirt. 'Just wet.'

Michelle shook her head. 'They came out of nowhere. Everyone knows there are speeding restrictions on the river – they were going much too fast.'

'Oh well,' said James, looking at his wet trainers with a sigh. 'I suppose they'll dry pretty quickly in the sun.'

'I think I may have found a nest of some kind,' Mandy said, diverted from her wet clothes by the memory of the small hole in the riverbank. 'It looked like something was living in it, from what I could see.'

'Well spotted,' said Michelle, making a careful note of the position of the hole. 'We'll check it out with the film crew. Even if it's not the voles, something may be living there.'

For the next hour, the three of them combed the riverbank for other signs of wildlife. Mandy pointed out the weir where the herons fished. To their delight, a young heron was standing like a statue by the edge of the weir, its long sharp beak angled down towards the water as it waited patiently for a fish.

Michelle had made over ten pages of notes by the time she checked her watch. 'I've got a meeting with my producer in about an hour, so I've got to go,' she said regretfully. 'Would you like a lift back to Welford?'

'We'll walk, thanks,' said James.

'We'll keep looking for that kingfisher, and the voles too,' Mandy added.

'We've done some great work today,' said

Michelle warmly. 'I'll be coming down here with the film crew later this week, to get some preliminary footage. Give me a call if you see anything else you think we could use.'

Mandy and James waved until Michelle's car had disappeared. At last, they turned back to the river. Mandy was about to follow James when she heard a slight movement behind her. Turning round, she let out a startled gasp. The rabbit they had seen yesterday was sitting a little way down the path, watching them.

'It's back!' said James in amazement.

As soon as it became aware that they'd seen it, the rabbit flicked one ear and shot sideways into the undergrowth.

'We've got to catch it this time, James,' Mandy said urgently, squatting down on her heels and peering into the grass. 'I don't think it's safe out here on the riverbank.'

'Shame we haven't got Blackie this time,' said James, bending down beside Mandy and hunting around with her.

'Well, Blackie wasn't much help yesterday, was he?' Mandy pointed out. 'Sshh, it might come out again.'

Just as Mandy's muscles began to cramp, there was a quick rustle at her feet. The rabbit emerged on to the path – this time, right in front of them. It shook its head casually, and raised one dusty back leg to scratch itself behind its long black ear.

'What's wrong with its eye?' whispered James.

Mandy reached out very slowly. The rabbit stared at her. Now that Mandy was close enough, she could see what James meant about the rabbit's eye. It had almost completely closed up. The lid looked puffy and red, and something yellowish was oozing out of one corner.

Mandy stretched out her hand a little further. 'Oh, you poor thing!' she said with concern. 'Come on, come to me.'

The rabbit watched Mandy's hand with its one good eye . . . and dodged swiftly to one side.

Mandy tried again, reaching out with both hands. But, again, the rabbit hopped sideways, its black nose twitching and its whiskers trembling.

'We've got to catch it and take a closer look at that eye,' Mandy said in frustration. She could see that the rabbit was trembling all over. 'Come on, we're not going to hurt you,' she coaxed in a gentle voice.

The rabbit's head was cocked on one side. Its nose twitched cautiously, but it didn't run off any further. Mandy wondered for a moment if it actually *wanted* to be caught. Did it understand they wanted to help it? And then the rabbit took off, straight down the path.

'Follow it!' Mandy hissed to James, breaking into a run.

The rabbit slowed down, almost as if it was waiting for them, then it bounded casually along the path, its white tail and feet flashing with every lollop. Mandy and James followed carefully.

'Look where it's going!' said James in astonishment.

Mandy watched, amazed, as the rabbit turned sharply off the path, straight up the ramp of the brightly painted barge they had seen yesterday. It hopped confidently on to the deck, where it promptly vanished through the cabin door.

Mandy stopped, her heart sinking. She remembered very clearly how cross the old man had been when they had disturbed him yesterday. 'Of all the boats it could have chosen!' she groaned.

'It must live there,' said James.

Mandy frowned. 'Maybe. Anyway, the most

important thing is that we catch it and look at its eye.'

'Are you sure you want to face that man again?' James asked cautiously.

A look of determination crossed Mandy's face. 'That rabbit's eye looked really bad,' she said. 'We've got to talk to him, find out if he's the owner. Maybe he hasn't noticed the infection.'

She put her foot tentatively on the gangplank. The wood gave a threatening creak. With a swift movement, Mandy stepped up on to the small front deck of the barge.

She looked around to see if she could spot the rabbit. The deck wasn't very big. The first thing Mandy noticed was another kingfisher painted on the cabin door, even more lifelike than the one on the side of the barge. The fish in its beak looked so real that Mandy could have sworn it was wriggling.

'Hello?' she called. 'Is there anyone here?'

BANG! The cabin door flew back on its hinges with a tremendous crash. James and Mandy both nearly jumped out of their skins.

'You again?' said the old man in disgust. 'Come to poke around, have you? Get off my boat!'

Three

'We've come about—' Mandy began.

'Didn't you hear me the first time?' The old man took a step towards Mandy. 'Clear off and leave me alone!'

Mandy took a step back. 'It's about your—' she tried again.

The old man seized an old broom that was leaning beside the cabin door and brandished it at Mandy. 'Go on, clear off!' He pushed the head of the broom angrily across the deck.

Mandy tried one more time. 'It's about your rabbit—'

The old man didn't seem to hear. 'For the last time, clear off!' he growled.

'Come on, Mandy,' James called from the towpath. 'It's no use!'

Mandy knew she was defeated. She backed towards the gangplank. The old man followed her suspiciously, still waving the broom. Then – BANG! The cabin door slammed shut again as he ducked back inside.

'He didn't have to bang the door so loudly,' sighed James. 'We got the message.'

'I'm not giving up,' Mandy said fiercely. She stood on tiptoe and peered along the deck of the *Halcyon*. There were neatly coiled ropes stowed under the seats on the tiny front deck, gleaming paint and not a speck of dust. But there was no sign of the rabbit at all.

'It's not there,' she said at last. 'At least, not as far as I can see. It must be in the cabin.'

'What did I tell you?' said James. 'The rabbit obviously lives there. It looked really at home on that boat. How many other rabbits do you know who would go up a gangplank like that? The rabbit must be the old man's pet.'

'Yes, but it needs help,' Mandy said miserably.

'Oh, why wouldn't he listen?'

'He was just a bit upset,' said James, trying to cheer Mandy up. 'No one ever listens when they're upset.'

'A vet needs to see that rabbit's eye or it could go blind,' said Mandy, her brow furrowed with determination. 'I'm going to come back here again, when he's calmed down a bit. I mean it!'

When Mandy and James got back to Animal Ark, old Walter Pickard was sitting in the surgery waiting room.

'Hello, you two,' he said, his lined face breaking into a wide smile. 'Have you been enjoying the sunshine?'

At that moment, Adam Hope stepped out of the operating theatre, stripping off his surgical gloves. 'Back already? Run out of provisions, did you?' he teased. He turned to Walter Pickard. 'Emily's just attending to Scraps, Walter. She'll be through in two ticks.'

Mandy looked at Walter, suddenly concerned. 'What's wrong with Scraps, Walter?' Scraps was one of Walter's three cats – a gentle old ginger cat who spent most of her time sunning herself on Walter's porch.

Walter smiled. 'Nothing that your mum and dad can't fix. She got her eye badly scratched last night – must have got caught in some brambles on a mouse hunt. It's been closed up all day, and she's been miserable about it, I can tell you.'

'Oh well, at least it's not too serious,' Mandy said, sinking into one of the waiting-room chairs. 'You know that rabbit we saw yesterday, Dad?' she said.

'Did you see it again?' asked Adam Hope.

'Yes. It's got a really sore eye, too,' Mandy said gloomily. 'We think we found its owner, but he wasn't interested in bringing the rabbit in for a check-up.'

Adam Hope frowned.

James spoke up. 'It wasn't so much that he wasn't *interested*. He just didn't listen to anything Mandy said. It was like talking to a brick wall.'

'Oh?' said Walter, sounding interested. 'Who was this, then?'

'An old man who lives on a barge down the river,' Mandy sighed. 'He got so angry, he practically swept me right off the deck!'

At that moment, Emily Hope appeared in the door of the operating theatre, holding a groggy ginger cat with a white bandage over one eye and a plastic collar round her neck.

Walter looked up hopefully. 'How is she?'

'Fine, Walter,' Mrs Hope said gently, stroking Scraps's ginger head. Scraps gave a feeble purr. 'She's just a bit woozy right now. She'll have to wear that patch on her eye for a few days, then she'll be as right as rain.'

Walter took Scraps gratefully in his arms. 'Lovely job,' he said. 'Your mum's a marvel, Mandy.'

Scraps shook her head with a small mew.

Walter stroked her again. 'None of your fussing, Scraps,' he said severely. 'That collar is going to stay on till your eye is better.' He smiled at Mandy again. 'Your mum could fix that rabbit's eye in a flash, I bet.'

'You saw the rabbit again, did you?' Mrs Hope guessed. 'What was wrong with its eye?'

Once again, James and Mandy told their story.

Walter listened intently, until Mandy got to the part where they followed the rabbit on to the barge. 'Did you see a name on the barge?' he asked with interest, gently putting Scraps into her travelling basket and fastening the door.

'Yes, it was Hal something,' Mandy replied. 'It had a picture of a kingfisher on it.'

'The *Halcyon*?' said Walter, looking up from the travelling basket.

'Yes, that was it,' agreed James. 'Why, do you know it?'

'I do indeed,' said Walter thoughtfully. 'Stanley Hopkins lives on it.'

Mrs Hope finished scrubbing her hands at the surgery sink and came out to join them. 'How do you know Stanley Hopkins, Walter?' she asked.

'We were at school together,' Walter said, remembering. 'We got into some scrapes, I can tell you.' He chuckled.

'So he's from round here, then?' Mandy asked.

'He's Welford born and bred,' Walter told her. 'Left the area to work on the barges, as I recall. When he retired, he came back here with his boat. Lives here pretty much permanently now, except for the odd jaunt up and down the river when he feels like it. Did you see Bess with him?'

'Bess?' echoed James, puzzled. 'We didn't see anyone else on the boat.'

'Bess is his dog,' Walter explained.

'There wasn't a dog,' Mandy said, shaking her head. 'We'd have remembered.'

Another mew floated up from Scraps's travelling basket.

Walter stood up, and took the handle of the travelling basket in one of his large hands. 'I must be off,' he said. 'Scraps'll tear the basket to pieces in a minute. Thanks so much, Emily. You've done a fine job.'

'Walter, you wouldn't come down to the river with us to talk to Mr Hopkins, would you?' Mandy said suddenly. 'You see, I don't think he'll ever listen to us, and his rabbit needs help. And since you know him, well, maybe . . .'

Walter stopped in the doorway of Animal Ark. 'I've not seen Stanley in a while,' he mused. 'Might be nice to have a bit of a catch-up. Why not?'

Mandy felt very relieved. 'When can we go?' she asked excitedly. 'How about this afternoon?'

There was another yowl from Scraps's travelling basket.

'I'll have to take Scraps home first,' said Walter, 'but I can think of worse things to do of an afternoon than have a stroll along the river.'

'Let's go after lunch,' Mandy suggested. 'With your help, we might be able to persuade Mr Hopkins to bring his rabbit into Animal Ark!'

In the sunny Animal Ark garden, Mandy ate the last tomato on her plate and washed it down with a mouthful of lemonade.

'Steady on,' said Adam Hope mildly, scooping up a forkful of pasta salad. 'You'll get indigestion.'

'We're meeting Walter in half an hour at the Fox and Goose, and James wants to collect Blackie first,' Mandy explained, wiping her mouth and pushing back her chair. 'Thanks for the lunch, Mum – see you later. Coming, James?'

James ate one more mouthful of the pasta salad he'd heaped on his plate, and stood up.

Mr Hope shook his head in amusement. 'I'm amazed you're still friends with Mandy, James,' he said. 'I don't think I can remember the last time she let you finish a meal in peace!'

'Well, we all know what Mandy's like when there's an animal in trouble,' said Emily Hope with a smile.

James looked at the rest of his lunch. 'I'm full, really,' he said. 'It was lovely, thanks.'

Mandy led the way inside. She hunted around the surgery until she found what she was looking for – one of the Hopes' spare travelling baskets. 'Let's line the basket with newspaper, and put in a few carrots,' she said, showing James. 'We'll bring the rabbit straight back here this afternoon.'

'You're very sure we'll get it this time,' remarked James, falling into step with Mandy as they walked into the village towards James's house.

'Oh, yes,' Mandy said confidently. 'Mr Hopkins will be fine when he sees us with Walter, I know it.'

They collected Blackie, and made their way to the Fox and Goose. By now, Mandy was running so fast that James had difficulty keeping up, even with Blackie towing him along.

Walter was waiting for them, an old tweed cap shading his eyes from the bright sun. They piled into Walter's car, with Blackie panting between them in the back seat, and set off for the river.

'Did you know Mr Hopkins well, Walter?' Mandy asked, scratching Blackie's ears.

'Stanley and I were very close in those days,' Walter told her as they drove along. 'Thick as thieves, our teacher used to say! Stanley was a bit restless, even back then. That's why he went to work on the barges. He wanted to travel and see the country, he said. But even the restless ones come home in the end.'

Mandy closed her eyes, feeling the cool breeze rush on to her face from the open window. She opened them again when she heard the distinctive crunch of gravel as Walter swung into the riverside car park.

Together, they walked down the short stretch of towpath to where the *Halcyon* was moored. Its colours looked brighter than ever in the sunshine.

The white-haired man was sitting in a chair on the deck, his face tipped up to the warmth of the sun.

'Afternoon, Stanley,' called Walter.

Stanley's weather-beaten face started to break into a smile. But he frowned when he saw Mandy and James waiting on the towpath.

'How've you been keeping?' said Walter quickly. 'These two are with me. Don't mind them.'

Stanley grunted. 'Well, as long as they keep that dog of theirs under control. So what are you here for, Walter Pickard?'

'These two had a question for you,' said Walter, pulling his cap down further to shade his eyes from the glare of the river. 'Mandy here is from the veterinary surgery up in Welford. This young lad is James, a friend of hers.'

'Well, what is it?' asked Stanley, sounding a bit impatient.

'It's about your rabbit,' Mandy began, determined to stand her ground this time.

Stanley leaped to his feet so fast that James

instinctively took a step back from the edge of the path. 'Bunny's the word you'll be wanting,' Stanley growled. 'I'll not hear that other word around my boat, if you please. It's unlucky for sailors.'

Mandy looked at James, puzzled. Then she tried again. 'Well, about your bunny, then.'

Stanley sat down again. His brow furrowed. 'What bunny would that be?'

'The one on your barge,' said James.

Stanley snorted. 'I don't have a bunny on my barge, and I hope that I never will!'

Four

Mandy was dumbstruck. She hadn't been expecting him to say that! 'But . . . we saw it,' she faltered.

'Not on my barge, you didn't,' said Stanley decisively. 'I'll have nothing to do with the creatures. They're bad luck on boats.'

'Bad luck?' echoed Mandy. How could a beautiful animal like a rabbit be bad luck?

Stanley nodded. 'Especially when you call them by that other name of theirs. Worst possible luck on a boat.'

'Really?' said James, intrigued. 'Why?'

'They eat through things,' Stanley said darkly. 'Rigging, for one. A bunny could eat right through a boat and sink it, mark my words.'

It was almost funny, except for the serious look on the old man's face. Mandy had no doubt that he believed every word of what he was saying.

'Honestly, Mr Hopkins, we did see a rab— er, bunny on your barge,' said Mandy. 'Didn't we, James?'

James nodded. There was no question about it. 'It hopped up your gangplank this morning,' he said.

'Couldn't we look around?' Mandy begged. 'We'll be very quick. We think it's injured, and we want to help it.'

Stanley opened his mouth, but Walter spoke first.

'Now Stanley, how about a cup of tea?' he suggested. 'I've come down here for a bit of a chat, and you've not even invited us on board. That's no way to treat an old friend.'

'A cup of tea?' echoed Stanley. He looked down at Walter, Mandy and James on the path, and his eyes lingered for a moment on Blackie. 'Well, you'd best come aboard then,' he said at last.

'Can I bring my dog, Mr Hopkins?' asked James. 'Or I could tie him up down here, if you'd prefer.'

Stanley looked again at Blackie. 'Bring him aboard,' he said abruptly. 'So long as you keep him quiet. And keep him in the shade. Dogs with black fur feel the heat more. And no more of this Mr Hopkins, all right? Stanley's my name.'

Walter turned and winked at Mandy and James, before walking carefully up the steep gangplank and on to the tiny deck of the *Halcyon*. Mandy and James followed quietly, with Blackie bringing up the rear. Stanley disappeared down into the cabin, leaving his guests on the deck.

Walter breathed in the soft river air and closed his eyes. 'Nothing like the air round here,' he said. 'Makes me feel ten years younger.'

An old kettle whistled somewhere down in the cabin. Stanley reappeared, carrying four mugs of tea on a tray. He also had a dish of water for Blackie, which he carefully put down on the deck.

Walter was still looking up the river. 'I'd forgotten how beautiful it is down here,' he said. 'Remember the fun we used to have along these banks, Stanley?'

Stanley grunted, but his face softened. 'I had to

do all the rowing in that old boat of your dad's,' he said. 'You just sat back, enjoying it all!'

Walter grinned. 'I kept you fit then, didn't I?' he joked.

Mandy looked longingly at the cabin door. She supposed it was possible the rabbit wasn't here. Maybe it had jumped off the boat again, some time over lunch. If that was the case, they were wasting their time.

Stanley's face was hard again. 'The river's not so much fun these days, Walter,' he said bitterly. 'Rowdy day trippers everywhere, spoiling the peace and quiet! Dropping rubbish in the water, and on the paths. Bess used to bark at them . . .' He paused. With a faraway look in his eyes, he stared down at Blackie, who was lying panting at James's feet. It was as if he was remembering something from the past. Mandy's heart ached for him as she saw the sadness in his expression.

'Has Bess passed away?' Walter asked softly. Stanley nodded. 'I'm sorry to hear it,' Walter went on. 'She was a good old dog.'

There was a pause. Stanley looked up at Mandy and James. He cleared his throat. 'We'd better have a look for that bunny, then,' said, 'since you're so sure it's aboard – it's not something I want on my barge.'

Mandy jumped up. 'Thank you,' she said gratefully. 'We'll find it in no time, we promise.'

She hefted the travelling basket under one arm, and walked towards the cabin door. James and Blackie followed. Opening the door softly, Mandy peered inside. 'Look at that!' she breathed in amazement.

The narrow cabin was full of everything you'd expect in an ordinary kitchen, but in a much smaller size. Honey-coloured wooden cupboards lined the walls, and tiny chrome taps shone above the metal sink. The windowsills were bright with blue paint, and there was an old jam jar full of cow parsley on the sideboard. It was hard to believe that anyone actually lived there, because all the usual kitchen clutter was stowed so neatly away.

'Wow,' murmured James. He stepped gingerly down the two steep steps into the cabin, and looked around.

Blackie jumped down into the cabin beside James, sniffing into the corners and wagging his long black tail.

Mandy spotted a photograph hanging on one of the cabin walls. Going in for a closer look, she saw that it was a picture of a black Labrador, panting happily on the deck of the barge. 'Look, James,' she gasped. 'That must be Bess.'

'She looks just like Blackie!' James said in surprise.

Mandy thought about the way Stanley had looked at Blackie, up on the deck just now. 'Yes, she does, doesn't she?' she said thoughtfully. At the back of the cabin, Mandy saw a small door that stood slightly ajar. 'Do you think that's the bedroom?' she asked.

James walked over for a look. 'It's tiny! Come and see!'

Mandy couldn't believe how small Stanley's bedroom was. The bed slotted neatly against the wall, and there was barely enough room to turn around. Everything was spotless. She thought of her bedroom back at home, with its untidy heaps of clothes. 'Pretty different to my room, isn't it?' she said with a wry smile.

James laughed. 'You could say that!'

Mandy looked around the small space with her hands on her hips. 'Now, if that rabbit – I mean, bunny's here, where is it hiding?' she wondered out loud.

It wasn't as if a rabbit had many places to hide down here. All the kitchen cupboards were firmly closed, probably to stop things falling out if the river got rough. The rest of the floor space was so small that a large black and white rabbit would stick out like a beacon. It was a real puzzle.

Blackie had settled down in the main cabin, his head resting on his paws.

'Come on, Blackie,' said James. 'We need your nose. Don't let us down!'

He patted his side and made encouraging noises. Slowly Blackie got to his feet. With James and Mandy urging him on, the dog started sniffing all around the tiny living area.

After a few moments, the tip of Blackie's tail began to wave.

'Keep an eye on Blackie, James! I think he's smelled something,' Mandy whispered.

Blackie's nose was firmly pressed to the rush matting on the floor of the cabin. Mandy and James followed him as he padded into the bedroom. He whined and sniffed in a circle, before pressing his nose underneath Stanley's bed. His tail was now a blur.

'I think we've found it,' Mandy whispered triumphantly. She got down on her knees and peered underneath the bed frame, moving as slowly as she could.

One bright black eye stared back at her.

'Is it there?' asked James with excitement, trying to get a look.

'Yes,' whispered Mandy. 'Shh, you'll scare it. Can you grab hold of Blackie's collar? Just in case the bunny makes a run for it.'

James took a firm hold of Blackie's collar and led him back into the main cabin. Then he came back, shutting the bedroom door carefully behind him.

As Mandy's eyes grew used to the darkness under the bed, she could see that the rabbit was busily eating something. On closer inspection, she could see that it was chewing the floor matting, nibbling a frayed edge with great concentration. With an uncomfortable feeling, she remembered Stanley complaining that rabbits were bad luck because they ate everything on board. But the poor thing was probably very hungry!

Mandy had an idea. 'Pass me one of those carrots in the travelling basket, will you, James?' she asked, keeping her voice as quiet as she could.

James quickly obliged.

Mandy held out the carrot temptingly. 'Come along, bunny,' she coaxed, waving the carrot from side to side.

The rabbit stopped nibbling the flooring and stared hard at Mandy with its one good eye. Then

its black and white nose started twitching, and its whiskers quivered.

Mandy slowly inched backwards. The rabbit followed her, stretching its neck to sniff at the carrot in front of it.

'A little bit further, come on,' Mandy encouraged. She felt pleased – the rabbit was nearly within reach!

Cautiously, the rabbit followed Mandy's hand and came out from underneath the bed. Reaching out one more time, its nose grazed the carrot and its little jaws began to work. Mandy let it nibble for a few seconds, and then started gently stroking it with her other hand. The rabbit was concentrating so hard on the carrot that it didn't seem to notice. Then, very slowly, Mandy scooped her hand around the warm furry body and picked the rabbit up. 'Got you,' she murmured.

James came over for a closer look. 'It's got beautiful markings,' he said.

The black and white patches on the rabbit's soft fur were certainly very distinctive. It was white all over with uneven black areas.

Mandy looked carefully at its infected eye. It seemed even worse than it had been that morning. She looked down at the rabbit, which was still munching the carrot. 'I think Stanley is about to get a big surprise!'

'Well I never!' Stanley's eyes nearly popped out when he saw Mandy and James step out of his cabin with the rabbit. 'There really was a bunny!'

The rabbit had finished the carrot, and was suddenly impatient in Mandy's arms. It gave an experimental kick, and then another, shaking its head so that its long ears flapped around.

'It's a lively one,' said Walter with a grin. 'Best watch those claws, eh?'

Mandy held the struggling rabbit as gently as she could. 'It's probably still hungry,' she said. She looked at Stanley apologetically. 'It was eating your bedroom matting, Stanley.'

Stanley looked annoyed. 'There, what did I tell you? Why, the little monster could have eaten through the floor of my barge, and sunk us all!'

Mandy caught James's eye and raised her eyebrows. He quickly shook his head, as if warning her not to say anything. Then he pulled another carrot out of the travelling basket, and passed it to Mandy. The rabbit stopped struggling immediately.

Mandy took a quick look at its tummy. 'It's male,' she said.

Stanley didn't seem interested in knowing anything about the rabbit. 'Eating my matting indeed!' he grumbled again, staring at the rabbit with distrust.

'Well, if it doesn't belong to Stanley, it must be lost,' said Walter, taking a long sip of tea. He smiled at Mandy. 'Have you given it a name yet?'

Mandy thought hard. She looked at the river as it twinkled and danced beside the barge. 'Well,' she said slowly, 'seeing that we're floating in the middle of the river, there can only be one name.'

'What?' said James.

'Out with it then, lass,' said Stanley impatiently.

Mandy grinned at them all. 'How about Bob?'

Five

'Bob!' Walter chuckled. 'That's a fine name.'

'A fine name for a floor-eating tyrant,' said Stanley, still eyeing the rabbit with displeasure. 'You'll be taking it off my barge now you've found it. I won't have a minute's peace with it on board.'

'He won't eat any more of your barge now, Stanley,' Mandy laughed, cuddling Bob. 'Not when there are carrots on offer!'

James laid the travelling basket down on the deck and unbuckled the lid. Then Mandy tucked Bob safely inside. The rabbit immediately settled down on the dry newspapers, and munched at the remaining carrots.

'There,' Mandy said with satisfaction. 'Now all we've got to do is take Bob to Animal Ark, so that Mum and Dad can look at his eye.'

'The sooner, the better,' muttered Stanley.

Walter got stiffly to his feet. He held his hand out to Stanley. 'Goodbye for now,' he said. 'It's been nice, having a bit of a catch-up.'

Stanley shook his friend's hand. 'Bye, Walter,' he said.

'Bye, Stanley,' Mandy said politely. 'We'll let you know how Bob gets on at the surgery.'

'The less I hear of that boat-eating creature, the better,' Stanley snorted, leaning his hands on the rail of the barge as his visitors made their way down the gangplank.

Mandy looked back to wave at the *Halcyon* as they approached the car park. Stanley was still standing on the deck, his eyes glued to Blackie as he ran along the towpath. Mandy knew that he was missing his old dog. Her heart went out to the old man, and she waved extra hard before getting into Walter's car.

'Got that bunny strapped in safely?' joked

Walter, as he switched on the engine.

'Yes,' said James, holding tightly on to Bob's travelling basket.

'Then let's head back to Animal Ark,' said Walter.

Emily Hope straightened up from examining Bob on the surgery table. She gently stroked the rabbit's quivering nose, taking care not to touch his infected eye. 'Yes, I can see what the problem is,' she said to Mandy, who was standing anxiously beside her. 'He's got a grass seed in his eye.'

It was the end of the day, when the last of the Animal Ark patients had either gone home or been bedded down for the night in the residential unit.

'Will he be OK?' said Mandy. 'He won't go blind, will he?'

'No, nothing like that,' smiled Mrs Hope. 'It's a nasty infection all right, but we've caught it in good time. It's quite common but it can turn nasty if it isn't treated. Luckily we can sort this out easily.'

Mandy felt a great wave of relief. Bob was going to be all right! You never knew how deeply an infection had taken hold when you were dealing with a stray, because they might have been sick for a long time.

As if she were following Mandy's thoughts, Mrs Hope spoke. 'I may be able to fix his eye, Mandy, but you know the rule,' she reminded her kindly. 'We can't keep strays at Animal Ark once they're better.'

Mandy knew that. It was one of the rules at Animal Ark that was never broken.

'Perhaps we'll find Bob's owners tomorrow,' she said hopefully, smoothing the fur along Bob's spine.

'Perhaps,' said Mrs Hope, pulling off the pair of surgical gloves she had been wearing. She tossed the gloves in the bin and turned to the surgery sink. 'But if you don't, you'll have to find a new owner for Bob, and quickly. His eye will be better in a couple of days.' She washed her hands and put her vet's coat back on the peg. 'We'll operate first thing in the morning. It's a simple treatment and shouldn't take long.'

'Thanks, Mum,' Mandy said gratefully.

Mrs Hope smiled. 'Perhaps you and James would like to settle Bob into the residential unit.'

The unit was only partly full today. There was a groggy grey rabbit with a smooth shaved side, showing a small line of stitches. On the side nearest the door, a cat with a splint on its leg was carefully grooming itself. And a guinea-pig snoozed quietly in one of the cages at the back, its hindquarters wrapped in bandages.

'Is there anything I can do to help before I go home?' Simon, the veterinary nurse, asked Mandy.

Mandy and James related Bob's story as they found bedding and food for him.

Simon watched Bob tucking enthusiastically into a bowl of rabbit mix. 'Seems your rabbit has still got his appetite,' he observed. 'He'll be fine, you know. There's nothing to worry about.'

'Yes,' Mandy said with a sigh. 'Nothing to worry about for now. But what about Bob's owner?'

'Let's just fix him up, and then we can think about that tomorrow, OK?' Simon washed his hands, picked up his coat and jingled the keys to his van. 'See you in the morning.'

When Simon had gone, Mandy looked at James. 'Do you think we'll be able to find Bob's owners?' she asked.

'I don't know,' James said honestly. 'If bunnies

are bad luck on boats, Bob probably doesn't belong to anyone on the barges after all. But let's think positive, OK?'

Mandy opened the front door and waved James off. She couldn't help feeling worried. If they didn't find Bob's owner, what were they going to do?

The early morning sun streamed into Animal Ark. Mandy was sitting on a waiting room chair. She hadn't slept very well the night before because she couldn't stop thinking about Bob. Counting the chimes on the Welford church clock as it struck through the night, she had thought about everyone she knew. Would any of them take in a stray rabbit if they didn't find his owner?

James appeared at the door to the surgery, panting with the effort of cycling at top speed from the other end of the village. 'Has your mum operated yet?' he asked breathlessly. 'I came over as fast as I could.'

Mandy nodded at the closed surgery door. 'She's been in there for about fifteen minutes.'

Jean Knox bustled in, checking her watch. 'You two are up early,' she commented. 'What's the drama?'

The surgery door opened. 'This young bunny's the drama,' replied Mrs Hope with a smile. 'And the day has barely even started yet!'

Bob was fast asleep in her arms, his long hind paws pointing at the ceiling. There was a neat white patch of gauze on his eye, attached around his head with a bandage. It made him look like a pirate.

Mandy rushed over. 'How is he?' she asked, touching his downy fur with one finger.

'Fine,' said Mrs Hope. 'The grass seed had worked its way right into the corner of his eye. But it's out now, the eye is disinfected, and in a few days he'll be good as new.'

'Can he stay here while he's recovering?' Mandy asked. 'James and I will look after him. We promise we'll try to find his owner when he's better.'

Simon appeared in the doorway. 'How's our stray guest this morning, then?'

'Well, Mum's taken out the grass seed, so hopefully his eye will feel better soon,' Mandy told him.

Simon stroked Bob between the ears. The rabbit breathed softly, its nose twitching in its sleep. 'How long will he need to recuperate?'

'A couple of days,' said Mrs Hope. 'Are we expecting any more patients for the residential unit, Simon?'

Simon shook his head. 'No, we've no one else booked in today.'

Mrs Hope thought for a moment. 'OK, Bob can stay while he recuperates,' she said finally.

Mandy beamed, but Mrs Hope held up one hand. 'But when he's better, he'll really have to go.'

'Whoa!' spluttered James, as Bob gave a sudden, powerful kick. Soapsuds and water flew across the kitchen table.

'I don't think he's enjoying his bath,' Mandy grinned, holding Bob firmly as she soaped his dusty legs and back. The water was already brown with dirt.

Bob had gradually regained consciousness in the residential unit the day before. At first, he had shaken his head a lot, trying to scratch at his eye, clearly bothered by the bandage. Mrs Hope had put a plastic collar around his neck, and the wound had healed quickly. Now, two days after

the operation, there was only a small patch of gauze left on the rabbit's eye. Mandy and James had decided to bathe and groom him, before taking him back to the river. It was the obvious place to start looking for Bob's owner. Besides, the fresh air would do Bob good, and it was clear that he loved being near the water!

The phone started ringing, and Mandy ran to answer it.

'Morning, Mandy,' said Michelle Holmes cheerfully.

'Oh, hi Michelle!' Mandy beamed.

'Have you had any luck finding that voles' nest yet?' asked Michelle.

Mandy suddenly felt guilty. They'd been so busy with Bob these past few days that they'd almost forgotten about Michelle's project. 'We haven't been down to the river recently,' she confessed. 'We saw that rabbit again – the one with the sore eye, so we brought him home and Mum operated on him and now he's convalescing. It's all been a bit busy round here,' she added apologetically. 'But we'll check out that nest today.'

'That would be great,' Michelle agreed. 'Perhaps you could give me a call tonight, and let me know how you get on?'

Mandy scribbled down Michelle's number before saying goodbye. As she turned back to Bob, he tossed his head and water flew off the top of his ears, spraying the kitchen.

Mandy wrapped the rabbit in a dry towel. 'We'll find your owners, Bob,' she promised, looking down at the bunny.

'I fixed that travelling basket to the front of your bike, Mandy,' said James. 'I thought it was the quickest way to get Bob down to the river.'

'Good thinking,' grinned Mandy, giving Bob a final rub. 'Come on, let's go!'

The breeze was gentle as they cycled down to the river. Mandy tried her best to avoid the potholes in the road in order to give Bob a smooth ride. They parked their bicycles in the shade of a tree, and made sure that Bob was comfortable.

'Do you think he'll be OK if we leave him for a couple of minutes?' Mandy asked anxiously.

James peered inside the travelling basket. 'He's still got plenty of cabbage leaves,' he commented. 'I'm sure he'll be fine!'

They walked down to the riverside and headed quickly for the place where they had been hunting for nests earlier in the week.

'Here it is,' Mandy said suddenly, after a few minutes of searching the riverbank. She frowned. 'It looks different, though.'

Unlike earlier in the week, there was no sign of habitation at all. The soft clay of the river's edge had crumbled away, leaving the hole much larger and more unprotected than before.

'If anything was living here before, it'll have

moved out by now,' said James. 'The hole is too exposed, look. The mud has been washed away.'

Mandy felt very disappointed. She'd been looking forward to giving Michelle some good news that evening. Now it looked as if they'd have to start hunting all over again. They trudged despondently back to Bob.

'Come on then,' Mandy said with a sigh. 'Let's go and see Stanley. Maybe he'll give us a cup of tea. We'll need it if we're going to be hunting for Bob's owners this afternoon!'

They reached the *Halcyon*, to find Stanley Hopkins sunning himself on the deck again.

'Back, I see,' Stanley commented.

Mandy unbuckled the travelling basket and lifted Bob out. 'Look, Bob's all cleaned up. His eye is much better too,' she added, placing the rabbit gently on the towpath. 'We thought we'd bring him down to the river for some fresh air.'

'That's good,' said the old man.

Bob sat up on his hind legs and sniffed the air delicately, one front paw held slightly higher than the other. Then, quick as a flash, he hopped up the gangplank of the *Halcyon* and on to the deck, where he sat at Stanley's feet.

Stanley jumped up. 'Hey!' he said indignantly.

'He likes you!' laughed Mandy. 'Don't worry, Stanley, James and I are looking for Bob's owners today. We won't let him eat any more of your floor!'

Stanley stared down at Bob, who was sitting contentedly in a sunny patch on the shiny wooden deck. 'Do you think you'll find them?' he asked.

Mandy crossed her fingers, and held them up in the air. 'We've got to think positive,' she said determinedly. 'We could really use some good news today. We've just had a bit of a disappointment.'

'What's that?' Stanley asked curiously.

'We thought we'd found a voles' nest,' explained James. 'But the hole had crumbled away, and nothing was living there after all.'

Stanley nodded. 'Don't blame them. I'd have moved from that spot too. They've found a nice new place, though.'

It took a minute for the old man's words to sink in, then Mandy's mouth fell open. 'You knew about the nest?' she asked in excitement. 'You know where the voles are now?'

'Indeed I do,' said Stanley. 'They've just moved further down the river.'

Six

'But that's fantastic!' Mandy couldn't believe her ears. 'You really know where the nest is!'

Stanley sat down again, giving a faint smile at Bob as the bunny snuffled around the deck of the *Halcyon*. 'You don't live on this river and not know about the wildlife,' he said.

Mandy turned to James. 'We'll be able to give Michelle some good news tonight, after all!' she said.

'Michelle?' Stanley looked puzzled.

'Michelle Holmes,' said Mandy.

The old man's face stayed blank.

'You know,' said James. 'From *Wildlife Ways*?'

Stanley's frown cleared. 'Ah, that young lady on the radio?'

'She's on TV now,' Mandy explained. 'And she's doing a programme about the river. We're helping her with some research. She'll be so pleased to hear that we've found the voles.'

Stanley got out his pipe and slowly started filling it. 'But I've not shown you the nest yet,' he teased.

'Will you show us tomorrow?' Mandy asked hopefully. 'Please, Stanley. It would be fantastic.'

Stanley looked down at Bob, who had settled down in the shade under the bench on the deck and closed his eyes. 'That depends on whether this bunny of yours sinks me first,' he said.

Mandy held her breath as Stanley put his pipe in his mouth and lit the tobacco. He took two long puffs. 'I will,' he relented. 'As long as you're quiet, mind. Those voles have had enough bother already.'

'Don't worry,' Mandy assured him. 'We'll be as quiet as mice.'

'Or bunnies,' put in James, grinning at Bob.

*   *   *

The weather was cooler the next morning, as Mandy and James made their way along the riverbank. They'd arranged to meet Michelle at eleven o'clock at the riverside car park. In the meantime, they planned to speak to a few people along the river, in case they could find out something about Bob's owners.

Mandy looked down at Bob, who was hopping along beside her. 'The river air yesterday did him some good,' she commented. 'I'm sure we'll discover that his owners live on a boat, James. I mean, look at him!'

Bob definitely had a jaunty air about him this morning. He'd spent another comfortable night in the Animal Ark residential unit, and was full of confidence and energy. He followed Mandy patiently along the towpath, rather like the way Blackie followed James. Mandy felt sure that he wouldn't run off again, and so Bob's travelling basket had been left strapped to the front of her bicycle. Blackie had got used to Bob by now, and ignored the bunny as they walked along.

Mandy and James spent a long, fruitless morning along the river. The boat people were very nice, and told Mandy and James how lovely

Bob was – but no one knew of his owners. In fact, it had been just like Stanley said. It seemed they were all in agreement that bunnies were bad luck on boats.

They met Michelle at the riverside car park at eleven o'clock sharp.

'No luck yet, then?' Michelle asked, looking at Bob.

Mandy sighed. 'Nope. But I think the exercise has done him some good.'

Bob snuffled and tossed his head, as if he was agreeing with Mandy.

'Tell me a little more about Stanley Hopkins,' said Michelle as they headed down the towpath towards the *Halcyon*. 'He sounds like he's led a fascinating life.'

'He's lived almost his whole life on the river,' Mandy said. 'And he knows a lot about life down here. You'll like him.' She thought for a minute. 'Though he's a bit grumpy,' she added. 'He used to have a dog called Bess, but she died. I think he's lonely.'

'He used to work on the barges in the old days,' James said. 'I don't think he's lived on land for about fifty years.'

'And he really knows where the voles are living?' asked Michelle.

Mandy nodded. 'Yes. We might see some voles today, if Stanley can show us the nest.'

Stanley was waiting for them on the deck. 'Hello again,' he said.

'Stanley, this is Michelle Holmes,' Mandy said, introducing them. 'May we come up?'

Stanley waved them aboard while James tied Blackie securely to a mooring post. He watched Bob hop up the gangplank with interest. 'Still got that bunny, I see,' he observed.

'Long story,' said Mandy with a sigh. 'We tried to find Bob's owner on the boats along this part of the river, but haven't had any luck. But there are more boats further downstream – we'll check them out later.'

Stanley looked at Michelle. 'I always enjoyed your show on the radio,' he told her. 'I don't have a telly, so I don't hear so much of you these days.'

Michelle smiled at him. '*Wildlife Ways* has been doing well on the television,' she said. 'And with your help, we could have a great programme on our hands, Mr Hopkins.'

'Call me Stanley,' Stanley nodded.

'Stanley it is, then.' Michelle smiled, and looked around at the tiny, neatly kept craft. Mandy saw her eye fall on the kingfisher on the cabin door.

'Did you paint the kingfisher yourself, Stanley?' Michelle asked curiously.

'I did,' said Stanley. 'Mind you, my eyes were better back then.'

'I bet you've seen a lot of kingfishers in your time,' said Mandy.

'There were usually one or two about the riverbanks,' Stanley replied, nodding. 'But you had to be quick to see them.'

'Mandy saw a kingfisher the other day,' James said proudly. 'But we haven't managed to find its nest yet.'

Stanley pointed upriver, towards the clump of reeds Mandy and James had been exploring earlier in the week. 'They always used to nest in there,' he said.

'That's where we thought they were!' Mandy exclaimed, pleased to hear that her hunch about the nest was right. 'They must come back there every year.'

'Crafty devils, I never could find a nest.' Stanley smiled, remembering. 'Halcyons, they used to call them.' He nodded at the name on the barge. 'That's why I named this old girl the *Halcyon*. A proper symbol of the river.' His face was soft for a moment or two. Then his usual frown came back. 'Not so many halcyons about now,' he said. 'Not much of anything, in fact.'

Michelle sat down on the deck bench. 'We've noticed,' she said. 'In fact, we're having trouble finding any wildlife along this stretch of the river for our programme.'

Stanley snorted. 'Don't I know it!' he said. 'Look around you!' He indicated a patch of the river over by the far shore. Plastic bags and an old beer can floated in the scum that had collected among the reeds.

'Filth,' he said in disgust. 'Plastic bags choking the swans, dirty water killing the fish. There used to be a time when voles were a common sight round here. There were more nesting birds, and you could see right to the bottom of the river. Now look at it.'

As if to prove the old man's point, a motorboat roared round the corner. It flew past the *Halcyon*, leaving a murky trail of water in its wake.

'Hopefully our programme will remind viewers of how precious the river is,' said Michelle gently. 'Mandy tells me you know where the voles are nesting. Would you show me?'

Stanley was silent.

'Are you worried about people bothering the nest?' Michelle pressed him. 'I promise that we won't mention its whereabouts, if that's worrying you.'

'If people know about the animals that live on the river, they'll help to protect them,' Mandy added. 'I'm sure of it.'

'Why don't we use that as our angle?' said Michelle suddenly. 'It's perfect! We'll highlight the problems of poorly controlled tourism on the river, and how it affects the wildlife.'

'That's a fantastic idea!' Mandy said enthusiastically. 'It would make people think more carefully about the river, wouldn't it? Then maybe the wildlife would come back.'

Stanley still didn't look convinced.

Bob was getting bored on the deck of the *Halcyon*. With a flash of his tail, he streaked into Stanley's cabin and vanished from sight.

'I think his eyesight's improved,' commented Michelle.

'If it eats anything else on board my barge, that bunny's in trouble,' warned Stanley.

'He won't get far,' Mandy promised, making her way down into the cabin of the *Halcyon*. 'There's not very far to go, after all!'

Bob was waiting for them in the cabin, munching steadily on a carrot.

'Look,' said James, pointing.

The carrot had been placed in a food bowl with 'Bess' on it. The word had been lovingly painted around the rim in the same curling script as the name of the boat. Mandy guessed in a flash that Stanley had made the bowl himself.

Bob finished the carrot and stared up at Mandy and James for a moment. Then he hopped past them and back up on the deck. By the time they had scrambled up the steps and into the open air again, Bob was heading down the gangplank and on to the towpath. Then he started munching the lush green grass that grew a few metres further along the riverbank. He looked perfectly content. Blackie whined, his nose sniffing in Bob's direction. But he was firmly tied to the *Halcyon*'s mooring post, and couldn't quite reach the rabbit.

'Best catch him before he goes jaunting off again,' said Stanley, watching the bunny.

Mandy made her way down the gangplank. 'No sooner said than done,' she promised. 'And then can we go and see the voles?'

A red and white motorboat suddenly roared round the corner, sloshing a huge wave right across the towpath. Bob leaped out of his skin as he was hit by the cold water. He would have bolted into the undergrowth if Mandy hadn't swiftly reached down and scooped him up.

She held the bunny's wet, scared body close and murmured soothing words. 'There now, shh, you're safe.' Gradually, Bob's trembling stopped, and he burrowed into Mandy's neck for warmth and comfort.

'Another river hooligan!' grumbled Stanley, his face red with anger. He marched down the gangplank towards Mandy, and reached out to stroke Bob's trembling head with one finger. With determination in his face, he said, 'I'll help you with your television programme. If it sorts out folks like the ones on that boat, that'll be enough for me. You wanted to see the voles? I'll show you them.'

* * *

Stanley walked ahead of them. 'It's just along here,' he said over his shoulder. 'Stay quiet now. They aren't used to visitors.'

'Just as well you left Blackie tied up at the *Halcyon*,' Mandy whispered to James. They had left Blackie guarding Bob and the barge.

After a couple of minutes, Stanley stopped at the foot of an old willow tree. The tree's leaves swept down and brushed the surface of the river. He put his finger to his lips, and waved. Mandy, Michelle and James walked forward.

Mandy got down on her knees, and crawled quietly to the edge of the water. The bank was very low here. The roots of the willow tree jutted out into the river, providing lots of small nooks and crannies for sheltering wildlife. The water lapped gently at the fringes of the towpath, and small pebbles gleamed in the shallows.

Spying a neat, round hole about an inch above the water level, Mandy motioned eagerly to James. James got down on his knees as well, and crawled up beside her.

The edge of the hole was marked with tiny scratches, as if small claws regularly scrabbled in

and out. Mandy almost couldn't breathe with excitement. The hole was definitely occupied – she could hear a gentle scratching, and as she leaned further forward she caught a glimpse of brown fur in the shadowy depths of the hole.

Then, as they watched, a round, dark brown head peeped out of the hole. Its face was framed with a shock of fur, giving it a rather surprised expression. With a gentle plop, the vole slipped into the water. Entranced, Mandy and James watched the animal swim quickly and soundlessly round the willow roots and out of sight.

'Wow,' breathed James. 'That was *fantastic*!'

Mandy couldn't even speak, she was grinning so much. Carefully she got to her feet and moved away from the nest. She didn't want to scare the vole if it was planning to return any time soon.

'They've got young ones too,' observed Stanley, standing under the shade of the willow leaves with his hands behind his back. 'Must have had them as soon as they found this burrow. Tiny, hairless things, about the size of an acorn. I've seen them squirming about in there once or twice.'

'We can film the babies!' Mandy said, fighting the urge to jump in the air with excitement.

Seven

'So who do you think Bob belongs to?' asked Michelle.

They were back on the *Halcyon*, drinking tea. Mandy was sitting with the bunny on her lap, playing with his long, soft ears.

'Someone close to the river,' said James. 'That's where we found him, after all.'

'I've been thinking about that,' said Stanley. 'And I've remembered something. It may not be much, mind.'

'What is it?' Mandy prompted him.

Stanley took a sip of tea. 'You have plenty of

time to think on a barge,' he said. 'And last night, I was thinking about all the times I've cruised up and down this river. I was wondering about that bunny and where he could have come from. And something popped into my mind.'

'Go on,' said Michelle, leaning forward with interest.

'A hutch,' Stanley said.

'A hutch?' Mandy echoed.

'A great big one.' Stanley nodded. 'I reckon I've seen a large hutch in the garden of one of the houses downriver, when I've been sailing past. About a mile or so, not far.'

'Can we walk there?' asked James.

'Walk?' said Stanley, surprised. 'I suppose you could. But I was thinking more along the lines of a trip on the *Halcyon*. How would you like that?'

'What, now?' said Mandy hopefully.

'No time like the present,' replied Stanley.

He started heading for the cabin door. Just before he disappeared below deck, he turned back and said, 'Best bring your dog aboard, James, and while you're down there, cast off the mooring rope, will you?'

James leaped down on to the towpath. Cuddling

Bob close, Mandy watched as he untied Blackie and the *Halcyon*'s mooring rope.

Stanley's head popped back round the cabin door. 'Throw the rope on to the deck,' he called. 'And make your way up the gangplank. Be quick about it, though, or we'll leave you behind!'

With one swift motion, James flung the mooring rope aboard and hopped up the gangplank, with Blackie following closely behind. Michelle held Blackie's lead while James and Mandy hauled the gangplank up.

Stanley appeared at the far end of the barge. Mandy was surprised. She hadn't known there was another deck.

The old man noticed her raised eyebrows. 'There's another door,' he called across the top of the barge, which was decorated with brightly painted boxes full of geraniums. 'This is where the engine is. You probably didn't see it when you were down below. Too busy looking for that bunny.' He chuckled. 'How did you think the boat moved? By magic?'

Mandy grinned back.

There was a roar as the barge's engine turned over. Then it settled down to a steady throbbing.

Mandy could feel the boat trembling beneath her feet, as if it were a live thing. She held Bob more closely, in case he got scared and jumped out of her arms.

Stanley carefully manoeuvred the long barge until it was facing upriver. 'We're off!' he cried.

As the barge moved smoothly through the water, Mandy could see every detail of the riverbank. Bob seemed quite happy to be underway. He started wriggling so much that Mandy put him down on the deck. Blackie watched with one eye, but didn't move from his comfortable spot at James's feet.

With a shake of his head, Bob lolloped down into the cabin.

'Well, I'm blowed,' Stanley called with astonishment a few moments later, looking down at his feet. 'That bunny's come to help me steer!'

Mandy walked through the cabin and joined Stanley and Bob on the engine deck. The bunny was sitting on the bench with his front paws up on the rail, looking back down the river.

'Bob certainly looks very comfortable,' Mandy grinned. She could see the tiller now – a long metal bar which Stanley was skilfully moving from side to side, keeping well clear of the banks. 'How fast does the *Halcyon* go?' she asked curiously.

Stanley shrugged. 'Maybe eight miles an hour, top speed. I've never gone much faster than five, though. No need.'

Mandy sat down and stared over the back of the barge at the passing scenery. It was wonderful being in the middle of the river like this. You could see both banks – and what was more important, you could see the river life from a completely different angle. Small birds flew amongst the reeds, and moorhens swam through the calm, chugging wake of the *Halcyon*.

'See those ripples?' Stanley pointed. 'That's a grebe, swimming underwater.'

'But a grebe's a bird!' Mandy protested.

Stanley nodded. 'He's after fish. He'll be up for air in a minute.'

Sure enough, the smooth, arrowlike head of a great crested grebe popped above the surface of the river. Then, the bird shook its head and glided upriver.

'Did you see that, Michelle?' Mandy called in excitement.

Michelle lowered her camera. 'I certainly did!'

she called back. 'And I took a few good shots too. Stanley, we're getting some wonderful stuff here. The crew is going to love it!'

'There are some houses coming up here on the left,' James shouted from the front deck. 'Are they the ones you meant, Stanley?'

A line of whitewashed cottages appeared on the bank, the towpath running along the bottom of the gardens.

'Yup, they're the ones,' said Stanley.

Mandy ran through the cabin, and rejoined James, Michelle and Blackie at the prow. Stanley guided the *Halcyon* expertly into the riverbank, where she bumped gently to a stop. Without being asked, Mandy grabbed the mooring rope and hopped down on to the towpath, fixing the end to a mooring post.

'You're learning,' said Stanley with a nod.

Mandy smiled. 'Well, we can't have the *Halcyon* floating away, can we?' she said. 'James, can you fetch Bob? Quick, before he jumps ashore on his own!'

But Bob beat James to it. With one confident leap, he jumped down from the engine deck on to the towpath and set off towards the cottages. It was as if he knew exactly where he was going!

'I'll stay with Blackie,' Michelle offered, winding on her camera and jotting something in her notebook. 'I've got to get all this down for the crew tomorrow.'

Mandy, James and Stanley followed the bunny along the towpath towards the cottages. Bob stopped at the first gate, and sniffed. Then he moved on to the second, and the third.

'I think he knows where he is,' Mandy whispered in excitement.

'Humph,' snorted Stanley. 'Bunnies aren't that clever, surely? It's food they want, that's all. He can probably smell someone's vegetable patch.'

Bob stopped. Then he stood up on his hind legs, sniffing at a gate. Mandy followed him, and peered over the fence.

Sitting in the overgrown garden of a small pink cottage sat a large rabbit hutch. It was covered with mesh, which was coming away from the frame in one corner. There was no sign of any rabbits inside.

Mandy looked at Bob. The hutch was about the right size for a big rabbit, she thought. Had they really found Bob's owner?

'Go on then,' said Stanley. 'What are you waiting for, lass?'

Mandy looked up the garden to the front door of the cottage. Squaring her shoulders, she picked up Bob and walked up the path. The others stayed at the gate.

Mandy knocked firmly, and heard footsteps echoing inside the house.

'Yes?' The round, anxious face of a middle-aged woman appeared at the door.

'Excuse me,' Mandy began.

But the woman had spotted Bob. 'Oh!' she cried, putting her hands up to her face in surprise. 'It's Minstrel! Wherever did you find him?'

The woman was called Mrs Biggins. She immediately invited them all in for a cup of tea. Flapping her hands and fussing around them, she couldn't stop marvelling at the reappearance of the rabbit.

'Minstrel belongs to my son, Steve,' she explained, gathering tea things from around the kitchen. 'When Minstrel disappeared about a week ago, I looked and looked but I just couldn't find him.'

'Where is Steve, Mrs Biggins?' asked Mandy, helping herself to one of the chocolate biscuits Mrs Biggins had laid out on a plate for them.

'Oh, he doesn't live here any more,' Mrs Biggins replied. She looked a little sad. 'He's gone off to university. Minstrel stayed here with me.'

'Was he upset when you told him that Minstrel had disappeared?' James asked.

Mrs Biggins looked guilty. 'Well,' she said, 'to be honest, I haven't told him yet. I knew it would upset him. Besides, I still thought that Minstrel might turn up. He's such a resourceful rabbit.'

'He had a bad eye infection when we found him,' Mandy said. 'My parents are vets, so they cleaned it up for him.'

Mrs Biggins looked concerned. 'I noticed the patch on his eye. I'm very grateful to you for looking after him. Where did you find him?'

Mandy tickled Bob gently between the ears. 'He was wandering along the towpath, about a mile from here,' she said. 'He jumped on board Stanley's barge.'

'Uninvited, mind,' said Stanley gruffly.

'Yes, that sounds like Minstrel,' said Mrs Biggins with a little smile. 'He loved the water. Stephen used to take him out on his boat sometimes. That rabbit would stand at the prow like he owned it!'

Stanley finished his tea and stood up. 'Well, we've brought him back to you now,' he said. 'Thank you for the tea.'

'Yes, thank you very much,' said Mandy, reluctantly lifting Bob off her lap and getting to her feet. 'Shall I put Bob – I mean Minstrel – back in the hutch for you, Mrs Biggins? He might be safer in there, if he's thinking of running off again.'

'Just leave him here in the house with me. I'll keep an eye on him,' said Mrs Biggins, getting up as well. 'The mesh needs fixing where he pushed his way out last time. I'll ask my neighbour to sort it out.'

With a pang, Mandy looked at Bob one last time. She wondered if she'd ever see the adventurous rabbit again.

'Thank you, Mrs Biggins,' said James politely. 'Come on, Mandy. Stanley's waiting for us.'

Walking back towards the *Halcyon*, Mandy's heart felt heavy with unexplained sadness. Why was she feeling like this when they'd found Bob's owner? She should be feeling happy.

Michelle was waiting for them on the deck. She looked sympathetic. 'No luck?' she said. 'Never mind. We'll find a home for Bob soon.'

'What do you mean?' Mandy asked, puzzled. 'We found his home. He's there now.'

Michelle raised her eyebrows. 'Really?' she said. 'So why is there a black and white rabbit following you right this minute?'

Mandy whirled round. Bob was lolloping along about two metres behind them. 'But we left him with Mrs Biggins!' she exclaimed.

Mrs Biggins came puffing into view. 'Minstrel!' she called. 'Minstrel, where are you going?'

Bob cocked his head to one side and jumped neatly aboard the barge. For once, even Stanley was speechless.

'Oh, Mrs Biggins, we're really sorry,' Mandy said anxiously. 'We had no idea he was following us!'

Mrs Biggins drew level with the barge, and stopped to catch her breath. 'I don't know what I'm going to do with him!' she said despairingly. 'He's got a mind of his own. He'll run off again, I just know it.'

'Do you mean that you don't want to keep him?' Mandy asked slowly.

Mrs Biggins looked upset. 'It's not that I don't want to,' she said. 'I just don't think that I can. We should have called him Houdini, not Minstrel. I'm worried that if he escapes again, a fox will get him.'

Stanley was staring at the bunny with a peculiar expression on his face. Suddenly, he spoke up. 'I don't really care for bunnies,' he said slowly, 'but I can see that you have a problem, Mrs Biggins. And I think I might have a solution.'

Mandy looked up at Stanley in surprise.

'I wouldn't want to see this bunny disappear inside a fox,' Stanley continued. He cleared his throat. 'So I think the best thing all round would be for him to stay with me instead.'

Mandy couldn't believe her ears. Was Stanley offering to keep Bob for good?

'But this is only temporary, you hear?' Stanley warned, dashing her hopes immediately. 'It's still up to you to find him a permanent home, Mandy. And that's my final word on it!'

Eight

On the deck of the *Halcyon*, Mandy checked her watch for the hundredth time that morning. 'Where are they?' she said impatiently. 'Michelle and the film crew should be here by now. It's past nine o'clock.'

'They'll be here,' James said mildly.

Mandy stroked Bob's tummy as the big bunny lay full length on her lap. Bob gave a quick kick, and Mandy remembered that it was time to give him his eyedrops.

'Time for that bunny's medicine,' remarked Stanley, echoing Mandy's thoughts.

Mandy smiled to herself. For someone who didn't like rabbits, Stanley Hopkins was taking very good care of Bob. She got out the small bottle and lifted Bob into a better position. To her surprise, Stanley suddenly put down his mug of tea and sat next to Mandy.

He cleared his throat. 'Tea's too hot to drink right now,' he said. 'I'll have a go at these drops of yours, if you like. It doesn't look too hard.'

Mandy handed Bob and the eyedrops to Stanley. Stanley held the bunny gingerly with one arm, as if he was afraid he might break him.

'It's very easy, look,' Mandy said, encouraging the old man. 'See, I'll lift the gauze, and you just squeeze two drops into the corner of his eye. He's used to it now, so he won't wriggle. Well, not too much,' she added.

Stanley took aim with the eyedropper and squeezed. Bob shook his head and scrabbled with his back feet.

'Whoa!' said Stanley hurriedly. 'Steady on, you daft creature. I'm trying to help you!'

Mandy lifted Bob into her arms. Stanley looked relieved.

'That was really good for a first time,' Mandy

grinned, tickling Bob under the chin.

'Humph,' said Stanley, eyeing Bob.

'Here comes Michelle with the crew!' called James, pointing up the towpath.

'You're here early!' Michelle smiled in greeting as she approached the *Halcyon*.

'We didn't want to miss anything,' Mandy said, jumping down on to the towpath to say hello.

'These two are Bill and Terry, cameraman and sound operator,' Michelle said, waving towards her two companions.

Bill was tall and grey-haired, carrying a camera on one shoulder and a bag full of film on the other. Terry was the opposite – young, blond and slight, with a quick smile. Cables snaked out from his shoulder bag, and Mandy caught a glimpse of a furry microphone among the wires.

'Bill, Terry – these are Mandy and James, our research assistants. That's Bob the rabbit in Mandy's arms, and this is Stanley Hopkins.' Michelle finished the introductions. 'He's the one who told us about the voles' nest.'

Stanley shook hands silently. Mandy could see that he was weighing up these two new visitors, deciding whether or not to trust them. 'Know

much about voles, then?' he asked gruffly. 'You'll
not go disturbing them, will you?'

Terry laughed. 'I've seen a few in my time. My
family used to keep a barge on the river. We always
spent our holidays on the water. I loved it.'

'Did you?' Stanley seemed to warm to him
immediately.

'Bill loves the water too,' Terry went on. 'Only
he knows more about the sea.'

Within a few minutes, Stanley was chatting to
Bill and Terry as if he'd known them all his life.
Mandy exchanged a quick grin with James and
Michelle. They all knew that Stanley would do
everything he could to help them with their
filming. Now all they needed was some co-
operative wildlife!

When a light summer rain started to fall at the
end of the morning, Mandy and James cycled back
to Animal Ark for lunch. Mandy was now in the
middle of explaining the filming platform to her
mum and dad between hurried bites of sandwich.
'We helped Bill and Terry to set it up over the
river. It was really long—' She flung her arms out
to demonstrate, and knocked over the pepper

grinder. It fell on to the kitchen floor with a clatter, and Blackie retreated under James's chair.

'Steady on, Mandy,' laughed Mr Hope. 'We get the picture without you wrecking the kitchen!'

'How's Bob settling in with Stanley?' Mrs Hope asked.

Mandy grinned. 'We should probably call him Minstrel now,' she said. 'But I can't help thinking of him as Bob! He loves it with Stanley, Mum. Honestly, it's like he's spent his whole life on a barge. And Stanley loves his company. He's even built Bob a ramp down into the cabin! You wouldn't believe it's only temporary.'

'Do you think Stanley might change his mind?' asked Mr Hope.

Mandy looked thoughtful. 'Maybe,' she said. 'But he still talks about bunnies being bad luck.'

'There's more bread in the breadbin, Mandy,' said Mrs Hope, standing up and carrying her lunch plate to the sink. 'You can make some sandwiches to take back to the river, if you like. I presume you and James are going back to the river this afternoon?'

Mandy nodded, swallowing the last bite of her cheese and pickle sandwich. 'Yes, they're hoping to get some footage of herons before sunset. I'd love to see that. Oh, and the most important thing of all . . .' She paused dramatically.

Mr Hope looked interested. 'What?'

'They're going to be filming all night!' Mandy's eyes shone with excitement. 'They're bound to get some fantastic stuff – owls, foxes and maybe badgers. So, we were wondering if we could camp out? You know, so we could take turns with the film crew, and see what's going on. It'll be brilliant!'

'Dad's got a really good tent we could use,' James added. 'It's very easy to set up.'

'I don't see any problem,' said Mr Hope, nodding. 'So long as you camp near Stanley's barge, where he can keep an eye on you. What do you think, Emily?'

Mrs Hope grabbed her white coat from the peg and slipped it on. 'That sounds fine,' she said with a smile. 'Now, your dad and I have got to head back to work, Mandy – the appointments book is overflowing this afternoon. Camp near Stanley, don't get in the way – and have a good time!' She disappeared through the doorway and into the Animal Ark surgery.

'Your mum's right,' said Mr Hope. 'I think we're going to be really busy this afternoon. Camping tonight is a great idea.' He shrugged on his coat, and headed for the surgery. 'I wish I was coming with you,' he said, pausing at the door. 'But I guess I'll catch it all on TV!'

Mandy and James took Blackie back to James's house and collected the tent. James grabbed his shrimping net from the umbrella stand by the door.

'What's that for?' Mandy asked with interest.

James pushed his glasses up his nose. 'I thought we could check the sticklebacks, if we have time,' he explained. 'Numbers were down at half-term. I thought I could do a kind of PS on my project.'

Mandy nodded. James's project had been the best in his class last term. But it was typical of James to want to make it even better.

Back at the river, they found Stanley sitting on the rear deck of the *Halcyon* with Bob on his knee and an oily towel in his hand.

'We've just been tinkering with the engine, and we both need a bit of a clean up,' Stanley explained. He looked fondly down at Bob, whose nose had a smudge of engine oil on it. 'This bunny's the most curious animal I've ever met. He can't keep his nose out of anything, can you Bob, my old fellow?'

Mandy grinned. It was 'Bob, my old fellow' now, was it?

Down beside the weir, Mandy and James found the film crew in the place where they'd seen the young heron fishing with Michelle earlier in the week.

'I can't see the camera at all,' Mandy said in amazement, looking around her.

Bill laughed softly. 'Looks like we've done a good job, then,' he said. 'I've heard about your sharp eyes.'

'And of course, herons' eyes are even sharper,' added Terry, adjusting the microphone.

They waited quietly, watching out for a heron. It was amazing the things that you could see if you stayed still for long enough. Ducks dabbled, diving down under the green water. Dragonflies hummed around the reeds like small blue helicopters, and squirrels raced up and down the willow trees along the waterfront.

A young grey heron appeared on the far bank. It looked like the same one from the other day.

Utterly motionless, it stood as if it was carved from wood. It stayed like that for such a long time, Mandy wondered if it had fallen asleep. At last it lowered its head very slowly and relaxed into a strange hunched position. Mandy recognised the signs. It had spotted its prey.

The heron's beak shot out like lightning. But the bird didn't plunge into the water. Instead, it flew into the reeds on the bank and swept upwards with something wriggling in its beak.

'It's got a mouse!' James breathed in amazement.

Mandy wouldn't have believed it if she hadn't seen it with her own eyes.

'I've never seen that before,' gasped Michelle, her eyes fixed on the heron. 'Did you get that, Bill?'

Bill grinned broadly. 'Absolutely,' he said. 'I think we've just got one of our main sequences, right there!'

Michelle checked her watch. 'Perfect,' she said. She looked across at Mandy and James. 'We'll be filming at the voles' nest in a few hours, when it starts getting dark. Why don't you go and set up your tent? We'll see you later. Nine o'clock sharp, OK?'

The early evening sky was breaking out into a pattern of stars. Mandy lay back in the grass, staring upwards. On a warm summer night like this, she thought she'd be happy lying here for ever, listening to the sound of the river running past and looking at the stars.

After a quick supper of soup and warm rolls with Stanley and Bob, they'd found a perfect spot for the tent a few yards back from the towpath, sheltered by a stand of trees and in full view of the *Halcyon*. James had almost finished putting up the tent. It was nearly time to join Michelle and the crew.

Suddenly Mandy heard a lonely, eerie sound, high up in the darkness. She sat up. 'James!' she whispered, leaning over to the tent and tapping on the canvas. 'I think I heard an owl.'

Quickly James crawled out from behind the tent, a bag of tent pegs in his hand. 'What, just now?' he said eagerly. He stared up into the evening sky and listened hard. But the owl had fallen silent.

'Maybe we'll hear it again later,' Mandy consoled him. 'Come on! I don't want to miss anything.'

James hammered in one last tent peg. 'Done,' he said triumphantly. 'That's not going to fall down in a hurry.'

'Very good,' Mandy remarked, tugging experimentally on a guy rope. She checked her torch, and tightened the laces in her trainers. 'Let's hope that tonight's filming turns up something really special!'

'Shall we take it in turns to watch and sleep?' asked James, as they moved quickly along the dark towpath, following the beam of their torches. 'It's going to be a long night.'

The sounds of the river seemed amplified in the darkness, and Mandy was very aware of every rustle in the grass, and every splash of the river. 'Only if we promise to wake each other up if something exciting is happening,' she said. 'It would be awful to miss any action!'

They found the film crew beside the old willow tree. Yellow night-lights illuminated the bank, casting weird black shadows everywhere. Bill had set up the camera on the platform Mandy and James had helped to build that morning, and was focusing carefully on the nest. Terry was fiddling with an electrical board, adjusting the sound levels of the microphone.

Michelle saw them, and beckoned them closer. 'We're all set up,' she said quietly. 'Are you ready for a long wait?'

There was something really dramatic about night filming, Mandy decided. It was something to do with the shadows, and the way the river rippled quietly in the darkness. Small animals moved in the undergrowth, and the night was alive with sound.

James was the first to give in. 'I'll see you in a few hours,' he said to Mandy, yawning widely. 'Wake me up if anything exciting happens!'

At eleven, Mandy saw the first really thrilling thing – but there was no time to wake James. A snowy-winged owl swooped down only a few metres away from them and snatched at something in the undergrowth. Then it flew back into the trees, as silently as it had come.

'James will be sorry he missed that,' Mandy whispered regretfully.

Bill looked across and smiled. 'We caught the whole thing, don't worry,' he whispered back. 'James can watch it from the comfort of his own home!'

At one o'clock, Stanley emerged through the darkness, carrying two Thermo flasks filled with warm soup. Then James appeared, zipping his fleece tightly up around his chin. 'Go and get some sleep, Mandy,' he advised. 'You won't be able to see anything if you're tired.'

Mandy gave an enormous yawn. James was right, she thought reluctantly. She turned to Stanley. 'Will you be here at dawn?' she asked.

'I'll be here,' Stanley promised, settling down.

Mandy opened her mouth to speak. 'And we promise to come and wake you up if anything interesting is happening!' he laughed.

Mandy crawled wearily into the tent. She slept deeply until the first fingers of light pierced the canvas. In a moment, she was wide awake. Morning! Had she missed anything?

She rushed out of the tent, dragging on her fleece. The morning was dewy and cool, and mist was rising from the river. The sun hadn't risen yet. Hurrying along to the willow tree, Mandy took care not to break the glittering spiderwebs that criss-crossed the towpath.

As soon as she saw the film crew, Mandy knew that something was up. Michelle spotted her, and put her finger on her lips, signalling quiet. Like a mouse, Mandy tiptoed on to the filming platform, so that she would get a better view of the riverbank.

James was already there. He pointed towards the voles' nest, and Mandy looked.

Two adult voles were bustling around the mouth of the nest. Tucked into the hole behind them, Mandy could see movement and hear a very faint, very high-pitched squeaking. After a few more moments, the whole family appeared – four tiny babies huddled together in a warm heap just outside the nest. Their fur had grown, soft and dark and fuzzy on their small bodies.

Suddenly, the peace was shattered. With an explosive roar, a red and white motorboat raced into view, tearing up the river at top speed. It was the same boat that had soaked Bob the other day. A muddy rippling wave flung itself against the riverbank, against the voles' nest – and the whole family, adults and babies, were swept out into the churning water.

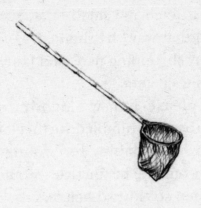

Nine

Mandy gasped in horror. 'Quick!' she shouted. 'They're going to drown!' Without a second thought, she jumped off the riverbank and into the water.

'Mandy, come back!' shouted Stanley. 'You can't swim out there, it's too far!'

'Well, what else can we do?' Mandy called desperately, wading further into the water.

Already, the voles' nest was out in the middle of the river. Mandy could see grasses and twigs swirling in the current, but there was no sign of the family.

Stanley was already running towards the

Halcyon. 'I'll fetch my small boat, see if we can reach them that way,' he shouted.

'I'll get my shrimping net!' said James, running off towards their tent.

'Hurry, please hurry!' Mandy watched in despair as the nest tumbled further out into the water. Were the babies too young to swim? Swimming would be instinctive – wouldn't it? But they had been so tiny, so helpless . . .

Mandy suddenly realised the quickest way to the voles would be on land. Her clothes felt heavy and wet, and her feet were sinking into the mud – she couldn't reach them from here. She turned around as fast as she could, and scrambled out of the river. Bill and Terry hauled her up on to the filming platform.

Mandy tore off her soaking trainers and flung down her heavy, wet fleece. She'd run better without them. 'They're floating downstream, we mustn't lose them!' she cried. Then she took off, sprinting down the towpath, trying to keep the voles' nest in sight.

'I think they're heading for the weir!' called Michelle, running close behind Mandy. Bill and Terry followed.

Mandy's heart turned to stone. 'The weir!' she gasped.

She heard the buzzing sound of a small engine. Spinning round, she saw Stanley and James powering downriver in Stanley's little boat, whose outboard motor was running at full throttle. She could see that James had his shrimping net. In comparison to the drama here on the river, sticklebacks seemed very tame indeed.

'They're heading for the weir!' Mandy called across the water, waving wildly. 'You've got to get to them first, or . . .' The lump in her throat threatened to turn into tears.

'It's OK!' Stanley called back. 'There's a patch of still water just before the weir, where the currents are sluggish. We'll try and head them off there!'

Mandy could hardly watch as the nest broke further apart, and floated closer and closer to the weir. Suddenly, she caught a glimpse of one or two tiny brown dots breaking the surface of the water. Were they the baby voles?

Stanley steered the small craft expertly around the broken nest, and brought it closer to the riverbank. His plan seemed to be working. The broken twigs and grasses bobbed on the waves between the boat and the bank. Any moment now, they'd reach calm waters and the voles would be safe.

Stanley brought the boat right into the shore, preventing the nest from floating any further downstream. James leaped ashore, his net in his hand, and scooped deep into the river. Carefully, he brought his net to the surface. It was filled with leaves, and twigs – and could Mandy see a vole?

'Are they there?' Mandy asked, hardly daring to breathe.

'I think so,' gasped James. Carefully he examined the contents of his net. 'Yes!'

Kneeling down, he quickly turned out the net on to a dry patch of moss. Two bedraggled bodies squirmed feebly among a collection of wet leaves and other river flotsam.

'There are still two missing!' Mandy gasped in panic.

James jumped back into Stanley's boat, and pulled his net through the water again. Mandy knew it was important not to touch the young voles too much, or the mother wouldn't take them back. She picked up one of the young voles as carefully as she could. With soaking wet fur, the tiny creature looked even smaller than it had in the nest. Then she started rubbing it carefully with a clump of soft, dry moss, until its fur stood out in little wet spikes all over its body. She was aware that Stanley was next to her, doing the same thing for the second baby with another clump of moss.

'I've found a third,' panted James, carefully placing another bedraggled baby vole on the moss. 'But no luck with the fourth.'

Mandy snatched up the net, and waded out into the river. Hearing anxious squeaking, she looked round to see the head of one of the adult voles slightly upriver, swimming around in anxious circles.

A small, broken clump of twigs bobbed into view. Mandy almost missed it. Then she noticed a tiny brown shape lying among the twigs. She swooped down with the net, and gently scooped it up. It was the fourth vole – and it was lying very still.

She waded ashore as quickly as she could. 'This one isn't breathing,' she said urgently as she tipped the little body on to the bark. 'What can we do?'

The first three voles were already starting to revive, and Mandy could hear a plaintive, hungry squeaking.

'I don't think you can do anything, Mandy,' said Michelle, placing a hand on Mandy's tense shoulder.

'We have to try,' Mandy replied stubbornly. She tore up another piece of moss and started rubbing at the tiny body. The little vole was absolutely

perfect, from the tip of its nose to each of the miniature black claws on its feet. It was almost as if it was asleep.

'We've saved three,' Stanley told her, his voice gentle.

Mandy's eyes blurred over, until she could hardly see what she was doing. Stubbornly, she kept rubbing gently at the little body. And all of a sudden, there was a tiny flicker of life.

Mandy's heart leaped. She stopped rubbing immediately. The vole stirred again. It was alive. She had done it!

'Well done, Mandy.' Stanley smiled broadly at her. 'Let's return these little ones to their nest, shall we?'

Mandy carried the four babies carefully in her T-shirt as they walked back towards the nest. James collected grass, moss and leaves – anything he could find which they could use to replace the ruined nest and give the babies a warm place to sleep. Mandy looked around for the adult voles, but she couldn't see them.

'Will the adult voles come back, do you think?' asked Michelle, as James carefully placed layers of the new, dry bedding in the hole.

'Well, we've been careful not to touch the little mites,' said Stanley. 'But there's no way of knowing how the adults will react. We'll just have to hope.'

Mandy leaned down and tucked each baby vole back into the nest. Suddenly there was an eruption of angry chittering. Surprised, Mandy looked up – and saw an adult vole standing alert beside the roots of the willow trees. Now that she could see it properly, Mandy was amazed at how large it was – almost as big as a squirrel.

Another furry brown face peeped round the roots of the willow tree and joined in with the furious noise the first one was making.

'I think they're trying to tell us that we're not welcome,' observed James.

'There's gratitude for you!' laughed Mandy, standing up slowly so as not to alarm them.

The voles gave one or two more outraged squeaks, then disappeared into the water.

'They won't come back until we're safely out of the way,' said Stanley. 'Why don't you all come back to the *Halcyon* for some breakfast?'

'It looks like you've wasted a morning's filming,' Mandy said sadly to Bill, as they walked along the towpath towards the *Halcyon*.

'Wasted?' Bill echoed with a laugh. 'Nothing was wasted! We filmed the whole thing.'

'You did?' Mandy looked at him in astonishment. She had been so caught up in the dramatic rescue that she hadn't noticed.

Bill tapped the side of his nose. 'I've had plenty of practice at not being seen,' he said with a grin.

'Mandy, you're sopping wet!' exclaimed Jean Knox as Mandy squelched into Animal Ark. 'Whatever happened to you?'

It was the quiet time just before lunch at the surgery. Although Stanley had invited everyone to stay for something to eat on the *Halcyon*, Mandy decided to pop home and change. It was strange to think that after all the drama of the day, it was still barely lunchtime.

'I jumped into the river to rescue the voles,' she explained.

'Well, that explains it,' said Jean dryly. 'Now, your dad has just popped out for a home visit, and your mum is busy with a patient. I think your trainers, socks and fleece had better go outside in the garden, don't you? They'll dry quicker. Now, what's this about voles?'

Mandy recounted the morning's drama while she peeled off her wet things. 'And the adult voles came back to the nest,' she added happily, seizing an apple from the fruit bowl on the reception desk and sinking her teeth into it. 'We were worried in case they abandoned the babies,' she added through a mouthful.

Mrs Hope popped her head round the door of one of the operating theatres. 'Jean, is Simon around? I need some—' She caught sight of Mandy. 'Hi, sweetheart, you're back early,' she grinned. Then she noticed Mandy's wet clothes and frowned. 'Is everything OK?'

'Yes, but it's a long story,' Mandy said. 'The crew is doing some editing this afternoon, and then they'll start filming again this evening. Is there anything I can do round here?'

'Don't worry, Simon's got everything under control,' Mrs Hope said. 'You're camping again tonight, aren't you? Will we see you later?'

Mandy finished her apple. 'Probably not till tomorrow morning,' she said. 'I'll head back to the river once I've got changed.'

Mrs Hope nodded. 'OK.'

Mandy headed upstairs to change into some

clean clothes. She thought about Bob the bunny again. She was uncomfortably aware that with all the excitement of Michelle and the film crew, she was neglecting the all-important job of finding Bob a permanent home. She racked her brains, trying to think of someone who could take him in. It needed to be someone who had time to look after him. Bob got too restless when he was left on his own. Maybe someone who was retired. And they'd have to live by the river as well. Mandy couldn't imagine Bob being happy anywhere else.

It was no good. The only person she knew who fitted the requirements was Stanley himself.

She paused. Why not Stanley? She knew he blustered about not wanting a bunny. But when she'd seen Bob and Stanley together on board the *Halcyon* earlier, she'd sensed something special. It was to do with the way Stanley spoke to the rabbit, as if Bob was somehow human. If that didn't prove that Stanley liked the bunny, Mandy didn't know what would.

She tugged on a clean pair of jeans and hunted out a dry pair of trainers. The more she thought about it, the better it seemed. Bob obviously thought of the *Halcyon* as home already, and

Stanley liked the bunny's company. But of course, there was still the problem of Stanley's superstitious feelings about rabbits. It was so unfair. The rabbit hadn't brought bad luck – he'd brought *good* luck instead, and plenty of it.

With a flash, Mandy knew how she could put it to Stanley. What if she pointed out all the *good* things that had happened since they had found Bob? Stanley couldn't defend his superstition then, could he?

Down at the barge early that evening, Mandy began to put her plan into action.

'We've been having a great week since we found Bob,' she said, stroking the big rabbit. 'We even saved the baby voles – all four of them. Maybe he's lucky after all.'

'Maybe,' grunted Stanley, filling his pipe with a wad of dark tobacco. 'But a bunny's a bunny where boats are concerned. There's no getting away from that.'

Mandy kept trying. 'But good luck must—'

'Evening!' Michelle and the film crew were approaching the *Halcyon*. 'Can we come aboard?'

'How were the rushes?' James asked, looking

up from his wildlife magazine. 'Have you got some good stuff?'

'Fantastic,' grinned Michelle. 'We've brought back the tape, so you can watch it later. But right now, I think we're off in search of that elusive kingfisher. We'll set up by those reeds you mentioned.' She looked up at the sky, which was clear and still full of light. 'Conditions are good, so if the kingfisher appears the footage could be excellent.'

There was a distant throbbing sound coming from downriver. Within moments it had grown to a roar. With a sinking heart, Mandy realised that it was a motorboat.

The gleaming red and white craft raced into view, sending up an arc of water that glittered in the afternoon sunlight. Mandy recognised it immediately. It was the boat responsible for flooding the voles' nest.

Stanley recognised it too. 'It's them!' he cried, leaping to his feet and pointing with his pipe. Bob jumped off Mandy's knee in alarm and hopped into the cabin.

Stanley didn't seem to notice. All his attention was focused on the motorboat as it zoomed by.

'River hooligans like that shouldn't be allowed. Not if I have anything to do with it,' he said through gritted teeth. 'I'm going to put a stop to it – right now!'

Ten

The motorboat was already rounding the bend up ahead.

'What are you going to do, Stanley?' Mandy asked anxiously, following the old man as he ran through the cabin and on to the engine deck.

Stanley Hopkins' face was like stone. 'I've a word or two I'd like to say to them,' he muttered. 'Tearing up the river like that, injuring the animals and destroying the peace.' He pressed the starter button, and the *Halcyon*'s engine burst into life.

Almost as if he had been waiting for the sound

of the engine, Bob's inquisitive nose appeared at the cabin door.

'Come on, Bob,' Mandy coaxed, holding out her hands. 'Come and join us.'

'That bunny follows you around like a dog,' commented Stanley, watching.

It wasn't her that Bob was following, Mandy thought. The rabbit's bright eyes were firmly fixed on Stanley.

Bob paused for a minute, sniffing the air. Then he hopped up to the engine deck, and sat comfortably at Stanley's feet.

'That's it, Bob, lad!' said Stanley, giving Bob's ears a friendly tug. 'Ready for action, eh?'

Mandy grinned to herself.

'Cast off then, someone!' Stanley shouted. 'We're ready for the chase, so let's go and catch 'em!'

'But . . .' James's voice sounded uncertain. Mandy knew that he was wondering how an old river barge with a top speed of eight miles an hour was going to catch a motorboat. She was wondering too.

'No buts!' Stanley said firmly. 'I'll be off whether we untie that rope or not, lad. So quick to it, if you don't want us to be trailing that mooring post!'

'The *Halcyon* will probably go faster without us on board, Stanley,' Michelle pointed out. She swiftly untied the mooring rope and flung it towards James, who caught it and coiled it neatly on the deck. 'It's a shame,' she added. 'I've a feeling that this footage could be the best of the week!'

The *Halcyon* began to move.

'Will we see you later?' Mandy called to Michelle and the crew.

'We'll try and meet up with you further upriver!' Michelle called back as the barge surged away from the shore.

'How are you going to catch the motorboat, Stanley?' Mandy asked. 'It's much faster than the *Halcyon*.'

Stanley smiled at her. 'There's a lock a bit further on,' he said, urging the *Halcyon* to its top speed. The water churned beneath the hull of the barge. 'Chances are we'll catch up with them there.'

'We'll catch them, I'm sure!' James called enthusiastically from the front deck.

'Go and join James, Mandy,' said Stanley,

guiding the tiller with an expert hand. He glanced down at Bob, who was still curled up at his feet. 'This bunny here'll keep me company.'

'You like Bob, don't you, Stanley?' Mandy said carefully.

'He's not bad for a bunny,' Stanley commented.

Mandy had to be content with that. But she promised herself that she would bring the subject up again later.

The brightly coloured craft powered along as Mandy made her way to the prow to join James.

'It's like one of those car chases you see on TV,' said James with a grin.

'Except a bit slower!' Mandy laughed.

The shore slipped past surprisingly quickly. Mandy and James waved at the film crew, who were jogging along the towpath trying to keep up with the *Halcyon*.

Mandy cupped her hands to her mouth. 'There's a lock!' she shouted across the water to Michelle. 'Further upstream! See you there!'

At eight miles an hour, they soon left the film crew behind. Ducks scooted quickly to one side to get out of the *Halcyon*'s path, and coots watched placidly from among the reeds. They soon passed

Mrs Biggins's cottage, and then rounded a bend in the river.

There in front of them stood the lock. The sluice gates were wide and strong, and the mooring posts on the riverbanks were painted a bright, clean white.

Just as Stanley had predicted, the red and white motorboat was hitched up to one of the mooring posts. On the deck stood two figures. They seemed to be peering over the side of the boat, down into the river.

'I told you to look after it!' the man was saying crossly.

'I *was* looking after it!' the woman replied indignantly. 'It was you who bumped up into the bank. How was I to know . . .'

Stanley steered the *Halcyon* up alongside the motorboat.

'I'd better go and give Stanley a hand,' Mandy said quickly to James. She ran back through the cabin to the engine deck.

Stanley called across the water, 'Lost something, have you?'

The boat's name, *Opal III*, was printed in large gold lettering along the starboard side. *Opal III*'s owner was a tanned-looking man with a white yachting cap perched on his head and a smart dark blue blazer.

'Our lock key,' he said. 'Have you got one we could borrow?'

'In a minute,' said Stanley. 'I'd like to have a word with you first.'

'What do you mean?' The man looked surprised.

'Is there something we can help you with?' said his wife, a slim woman with a red sun visor perched on top of her curly blonde hair.

'There certainly is,' said Stanley. 'You can help me by showing some consideration for the river. I've never seen such bad driving in all my born days.'

'Well, I—' the man spluttered.

'It was your boat that was speeding down the river this morning, at about six o'clock, wasn't it?' Mandy put in.

'I don't see what that has to do with you,' the man blustered, his cheeks reddening.

'As people who care about this river,' said Stanley, 'it has everything to do with us.'

'Well, you were going too fast,' Mandy said. The memory of the bedraggled voles filled her with sudden temper, but she was determined to stay calm.

'I don't know what you're talking about!' The tanned man's face was almost purple. 'We don't go any faster than some of the traffic on this river, and that's a fact!'

'The film crew are here!' James called from the front of the boat, pointing up the towpath. Sure enough, Michelle jogged into view, with Bill and Terry puffing behind her.

'Found you!' Michelle exclaimed cheerfully. 'Have you managed to sort out the problem?'

The boat owner's jaw dropped. 'Aren't you that lady off the TV?' he said curiously. He turned to his wife. 'Look Susan, it's that lady who does *Wildlife Ways*! My name's Derek Porter,' he added, turning back to Michelle.

'Have you been filming something round here?' Mrs Porter asked eagerly.

'Yes, we have,' said Michelle. 'And we've got some really interesting footage.'

'What footage is that, then?' asked Derek.

Michelle looked back at Bill, who handed her his video camera. 'May I show you something?' she said politely.

'Of course!' Derek said in a jovial voice.

Mandy could see that he was completely starstruck. Michelle was very good at turning on her TV charm when she wanted to.

Michelle pressed a button on the camera, and turned the viewfinder towards the couple aboard *Opal III*. 'This is something we shot this morning,' she said.

Susan Porter peered at the viewfinder. 'What are those rat things?' she asked. 'In the nest?'

'Water voles,' said James, who had come to join the others on the engine deck. 'They're an endangered species.'

There was a sudden gasp from Susan. 'Derek!' she hissed, pushing her husband towards the viewfinder on the camera. 'Look!'

Derek did as he was told. Mandy watched as his ruddy face drained of colour.

After a few minutes, Michelle turned the camera off. 'We rescued them from the river,' she said. 'But your reckless driving could very easily have been responsible for the deaths of four rare river animals.'

Derek looked deflated. 'We're very sorry,' he managed. 'We had no idea . . . I mean . . .'

Bob suddenly popped his head over the railings of the *Halcyon* and twitched his nose at Susan.

'Oh, Derek, look!' Susan exclaimed, completely distracted. 'There's a rabbit on that boat! How sweet!'

'He got wet when you sped past yesterday too,' Mandy said. 'I'm sure you didn't mean it, but do you think you could maybe go slower in future?'

'Yes, right.' Derek cleared his throat unhappily. 'We, er, still need to borrow that lock key of yours,' he said. 'If you have one, that is.' He paused. 'And if you don't mind lending it to us?'

Mandy watched, feeling relieved, as *Opal III* motored away at a snail's pace on the far side of the lock. Stanley had moored the *Halcyon* away from the lock, leaving the way clear for other river craft to get through.

'Well, do you think they've learned their lesson?' Stanley asked thoughtfully.

'They just didn't understand that they were doing any harm,' Mandy said. 'They were really upset when they saw that film, you could tell.'

'Your footage really showed them, Michelle!' James grinned.

Stanley looked round at Michelle. 'Yes, it certainly did,' he said.

'Would you all like to see the footage as well?' Michelle asked, looking round at everyone.

They each took turns at viewing the morning's film. The drama was unmistakable. Mandy gasped aloud when the voles' nest was washed away, and felt frightened all over again. And the sight of the bedraggled babies drying gently in the sunshine brought a real lump of relief to her throat.

Stanley was silent when he looked up from his turn at the viewfinder.

'What do you think, Stanley?' Michelle prompted.

'Marvellous stuff,' said Stanley at last. He looked up and saw *Opal III* still moving carefully upriver. 'Who'd have thought it could have an effect like that?'

'That's the power of TV,' grinned Michelle.

'How much more filming are you going to do, Michelle?' asked James.

Michelle looked at Stanley. 'That rather depends,' she said slowly. 'I've got something to ask Stanley, actually.'

'What's that, then?' asked Stanley.

'How would you feel if we filmed you, Stanley?' Michelle asked. 'We need a human angle for this programme, someone who loves the river and understands it. With all your knowledge, you'd be perfect.'

'You want to film *me*?' Stanley grunted, frowning. 'Well, I don't know . . .'

'Go on, Stanley!' Mandy leaned forward with excitement. 'You'd be brilliant!'

'We'd follow you and the *Halcyon* around for a

few days,' explained Michelle. 'Interview you about the past, talk about how things have changed and what could be done to make things better.'

Stanley looked at *Opal III* again, as it disappeared around a bend. 'Well, if your film can make people change their ways like that before it's even shown on the telly,' he said slowly, 'I suppose I could give you a hand.'

Eleven

The sun was beginning to sink over the horizon, and the *Halcyon* was back at its usual mooring upriver from the voles' nest. The film crew began setting up their first interview with Stanley.

Mandy could see that Stanley was a bit nervous about the camera, which Bill had positioned on the towpath. He kept shifting in his seat on the *Halcyon*'s deck, trying to get comfortable. 'Not sure I like that lens poking at me,' he said grumpily.

'Just forget it's there,' said Michelle, helping Terry adjust the microphone. 'OK. Why don't you just tell us what brought you to the river in the first place, Stanley?'

Bob suddenly leaped on to Stanley's lap. Stanley stroked him absently, and began to speak.

Mandy felt time slipping away as she listened. She'd heard some of Stanley's stories before, but the way he told them to the camera, it was like hearing them for the first time. Bob sat quietly in the old man's lap for the whole interview.

'Wonderful,' Michelle said at last, satisfied. 'That'll do us for today. You and that bunny are stars in the making!'

Stanley picked up Bob and put him down on the deck. 'The bunny may not be here tomorrow,' he said meaningfully, looking at Mandy. 'Had any more thoughts on getting Bob a permanent home, lass?'

'I'm working on it,' Mandy said honestly. She still hoped from the bottom of her heart that she could persuade Stanley to keep Bob.

'How's that tent of yours bearing up?' asked Stanley, as they watched the film crew head off back to the car park.

'Pretty good, I think,' said James. 'We thought we'd light a fire tonight, maybe toast some marshmallows. Do you want to join us?'

'That's a kind offer,' said Stanley gravely. 'But I was thinking more along the lines of a proper riverside feast. Why don't *you* join *me*?'

As the sky darkened, Mandy and James helped Stanley to build a fire on a carefully cleared patch of grass beside the towpath. Blackie trotted around and helped them collect the wood, while Bob the bunny watched from the deck of the *Halcyon*.

Soon the fire was blazing, and six small potatoes had been wrapped in foil and tucked among the coals. When the potatoes were cooked, they filled them with butter and sprinkles of salt and pepper.

As James set the marshmallows to toast on the fire for afters, a large black and white shape crept into the flickering firelight.

'Hello, Bob, my lad,' said Stanley, reaching out a hand to smoothe the bunny's glossy coat. 'Come to join the party, have you?'

Mandy knew that it was time to ask Stanley if he'd keep Bob. It was clear that Bob and Stanley were meant to be together. But how could she broach the subject? 'Bob loves it by the river, doesn't he?' she began in a casual voice.

'Don't we all?' said Stanley comfortably. 'I hope that new home you've got in mind for him is near a bit of water.'

'Yes, it is,' said Mandy. She took a deep breath. 'In fact—'

Whoo-hoo, hoo.

'An owl!' gasped James, sitting up in excitement. 'Do you think it's the same one I missed the other night?'

'Did I ever tell you about the time we had an owl nesting in one of the coal barges?' said Stanley, leaning forward. 'Well . . .'

The moment had passed. There was no point in trying to return to the subject of Bob. Mandy decided to try again the following morning.

They sat around the fire for another half an hour, drinking hot tea and relaxing in the warmth of the dying embers.

'Right, time for bed,' said Stanley at last, climbing slowly to his feet. 'I reckon we'll all sleep well after the day we've had, eh? See you both in the morning.'

Mandy and James watched as the old man climbed aboard the *Halcyon*, with Bob following at his heels like a shadow.

'Maybe Stanley is changing his mind about Bob,' commented James.

Mandy brightened. 'Do you think so?'

James yawned and scuffed out the fire. 'I only said maybe,' he warned. 'Come on, let's get some sleep.'

Mandy felt like she'd only been asleep for a moment when something woke her. She was wide awake in an instant, and lay frowning in the dark.

What was it?

Thump, thump, thump.

That was it – a strange sound. She'd heard it in her dream.

Thump.

She prodded James's sleeping bag. 'Psst,' she whispered. 'Are you awake, James?'

'I am now,' James grumbled, sitting up and rubbing his eyes.

'Shh,' said Mandy, cocking her head on one side. 'Listen.'

Thump, thump.

'It sounds like someone banging on a door,' said James, sounding puzzled.

Mandy scrambled out of her sleeping bag and

pulled on her trainers and fleece. 'I think it's coming from the *Halcyon*,' she said. 'We'd better go and find out.'

They crept out of the tent and stood for a moment in the dark night, listening. The moon shone brightly through the branches of the willow trees, casting shadows on the ground.

Mandy nudged James and pointed at Blackie. The dog was still fast asleep, his nose tucked between his paws at the entrance of the tent. 'Some guard dog,' she whispered with a grin.

'Blackie's not trained as a guard dog,' protested James, as they ducked through the willows and on to the towpath.

Thump, thump, thump.

'It's Bob!' Mandy cried in amazement.

The rabbit was thumping insistently on the wooden deck of the *Halcyon*, his ears flat against his back and his whole body trembling.

'What is it, Bob?' Mandy asked in concern, climbing aboard. 'Is it Stanley?' She suddenly remembered that rabbits thumped their back legs when they sensed danger. A cold feeling of fear crept into her heart.

'Something's wrong,' she said urgently to James.

'Stanley!' she called, opening the cabin door. 'Are you in there?'

There was no reply.

James nudged Mandy. 'Look at the floor!'

Mandy looked. The cabin floor was gleaming oddly in the moonlight. She stepped down – and gasped with shock as her foot sank into cold water. 'It's flooded!' she cried.

Several centimetres of water had already filled the cabin. Mandy could feel the *Halcyon* listing to the right, and knew with a flash of horror that the beautiful barge was sinking. She waded across to Stanley's bedroom door, and hammered hard. 'Stanley!' she called frantically. 'Wake up!'

'What is it?' came a grumbling voice.

Mandy shoved open the door and ran in. 'Quick, the barge is sinking!'

'What!' Stanley suddenly sounded much more awake. Leaping out of bed, he ran into the main cabin and flipped on the lights. Nothing happened. 'The water must have shorted out the electricity,' he said grimly, looking around.

They all stared. Even in the moonlight, they could tell that the water was rising fast – there wasn't a bit of dry floor left.

'Come on, you two!' Stanley rolled up his pyjama legs and waded into the middle of the cabin. 'Buckets under the sink, saucepans – anything! Fill 'em up and start bailing!'

Mandy and James seized the buckets, and started filling them and emptying them over the side. Bob had retreated underneath the bench on the deck, where he continued to thump his back feet anxiously.

Mandy lost count of the number of buckets she filled as the night dragged on. Scoop, empty – scoop, empty – scoop, empty. It felt like hours. Her head felt dizzy with tiredness, but still she carried on. James and Stanley worked silently beside her.

At last, the worst of the water was cleared. Stanley had found a torch, which he switched on. There was mud and slime everywhere.

'I've got to find the leak,' he said urgently. 'The cabin is below water level here and if I don't find that leak fast, all the bailing in the world won't help us.' He started investigating each galley cupboard, scattering the contents across the wet floor in his haste to find the leak. 'Keep bailing,' he ordered, his voice muffled by the cupboard. 'Don't stop until I tell you!'

Scoop, empty – scoop, empty. The water kept coming. Mandy thought her back would break if she had to scoop one more bucket, when . . .

'Found it!'

A board had sprung loose inside one of the galley cupboards. Stanley hammered the board back into place. Then he hammered on a patch. 'I've got to go overboard,' he said. 'Find the hole from the other side too.'

'I'll do it,' Mandy offered immediately.

Stanley snorted. 'Certainly not, Mandy! I may be old, but I've not worked on this river for fifty years without learning my trade. I'll do it quicker than you. Put the kettle on – I'll be needing a hot drink when I'm through.'

Mandy fetched towels and blankets for Stanley, and James made a pot of tea. And at last, the old man climbed back on board, wet and exhausted. He gratefully accepted the steaming tea, and sank down on the bench with a sigh. 'Well,' he said heavily. 'What a to-do.'

'Are you OK?' Mandy asked anxiously.

'As good as I can be, under the circumstances,' Stanley replied. He looked curiously at Mandy and James. 'How did you two know about the leak?'

'Bob told us,' said James.

'Bob?' Stanley's eyebrows lifted in surprise. 'How can a bunny tell you that?'

'He was thumping his back legs,' Mandy explained. 'That's how rabbits tell each other about danger, you see.'

Stanley looked dumbfounded. 'Well I never,' he said. 'I never heard of such a thing in my whole life.' He looked around. 'Where's that bunny then? I want a word!'

Bob crept out from underneath the bench, and flicked one ear. Stanley bent down and scooped him up. 'Well,' he said again. His voice sounded choked. 'Who'd have thought that a bunny might save a ship, instead of sink one?'

'He's no ordinary bunny though, is he?' Mandy prompted with a smile.

Stanley gazed down at Bob in amazement, and shook his head. He scratched Bob between the ears. 'You know what? I think this bunny belongs right here on the *Halcyon*. For good.'

Mandy hardly dared to believe her ears. 'Then you'll keep him?' she said.

Stanley smiled. 'Reckon this bunny's the one that'll be keeping me!'

* * *

The soundtrack from *Wildlife Ways* filled the living room, and the credits began to roll.

'Fantastic,' said Adam Hope enthusiastically. 'Stanley Hopkins is a real star, isn't he?'

Mandy's dad had lit a fire in the grate. Mandy was lying at full stretch on the carpet, soaking up the warmth of the flames. 'Stanley's a natural,' she agreed with a grin.

'Have you seen his picture in here?' asked Mrs Hope. She waved the local paper. 'He's become quite a local celebrity!'

'Let's see!' Mandy scanned the article. 'Welford's own TV star,' she read. Stanley's smiling face stared out at her. Sitting on Stanley's lap was Bob, looking very much at home. 'There's a picture of Bob in here too!' Mandy jumped to her feet. 'I bet Stanley hasn't seen this,' she said. 'Can I take it down to him now? It's only six o'clock. If I take my bike, I'll be back before supper.'

'Of course you can,' smiled Mrs Hope. 'And send him our best wishes while you're at it.'

It was strange to think of Stanley as a celebrity, Mandy decided, as she put the paper into her bicycle basket. She hadn't missed a single episode of *Wildlife Ways* – and now they'd videoed them all, she had them for ever. She added a couple of carrots to the basket for Bob, and grabbed a handful of dandelion leaves from outside the door of Animal Ark – Bob's favourite. The evenings were much cooler now that autumn had set in, so Mandy put on her gloves and helmet, switched on her bike lights and set off through the dark.

Parking her bike in the empty car park, she ran on to the towpath. Strangely, the *Halcyon* wasn't in its usual spot. Instead, there was a dark green narrowboat she'd never seen before, with smoke rising from its chimney.

'Hello?' Mandy called tentatively. 'Is anyone there?'

'Yes?' A woman with a mop of dark brown hair popped her head out of the cabin door. 'Can I help?'

'I was looking for the *Halcyon*, Stanley Hopkins's boat,' Mandy said, confused.

'Are you Mandy?' asked the woman with interest.

Mandy nodded. 'Do you know where Stanley is? I wanted to show him something in the paper.'

The woman smiled. 'I've a note for you, if you'll

just wait a moment.' She disappeared below deck and brought back a letter. 'He said to give it to you if you came by.'

Mandy slowly unfolded the letter. 'Dear Mandy,' she read. 'By the time you get this, Bob and I will have gone for a jaunt. I'm not very good at goodbyes, so I hope this letter will do instead. We'll be back next spring, so see you then. With love from Stanley and Bob.' There was a muddy pawprint next to Bob's name, which made Mandy laugh.

'He always goes in the winter,' said the woman in a kind voice.

'He will come back, won't he?' Mandy asked anxiously.

The woman laughed. 'Of course! He's Welford born and bred.'

That was all right then, Mandy thought, as she turned round. She was walking back along the river when her eye caught a flash of turquoise in the half-light. She gasped with surprise. A kingfisher darted past, and sat for an instant on a bare twig, its glossy blue head tilted cheekily to one side. Then it flew on, into some reeds and out of sight.

After a moment, Mandy noticed something fluttering on a bramble. Bending down, she saw that it was a tuft of silky black and white rabbit fur. She reached out and carefully untangled it from the thorns. Then she put it in her pocket with a smile. It would be spring again soon, and Stanley and Bob would return.

LEOPARD AT THE LODGE
Animal Ark in South Africa

Lucy Daniels

A family trip to South Africa means an amazing adventure for Mandy and James. They can't wait to go on safari!

It's their first week in Africa, and Mandy and James are hoping to see Leela, a leopard raised by big cat expert Sandie Howard and now released into the wild. Leela has recently had cubs, so when her tracking device goes out of range, everyone is concerned. Then Leela is found drugged and alone. What has happened to her cubs? Can Mandy and James reunite them with their mother before it's too late?

GIRAFFE IN A JAM
Animal Ark in South Africa

Lucy Daniels

A family trip to South Africa means an amazing adventure for Mandy and James. They can't wait to go on safari!

Mandy, James and their friend Levina are watching giraffes at a waterhole when Mandy spots one in trouble. Its legs are splayed to drink and it doesn't seem able to right itself. If the giraffe can't get back on its feet, it will become prey to prowling lions. Levina says they must let nature take its course, but Mandy notices a young giraffe waiting alongside the injured adult. Surely they can't just leave a mother and her baby to die?

HIPPO IN A HOLE
Animal Ark in South Africa

Lucy Daniels

A family trip to South Africa means an amazing adventure for Mandy and James. They can't wait to go on safari!

A violent storm causes chaos at the lodge where Mandy and James are staying. When they go outside the resort to check on the damage, they find a mother hippo in distress, standing guard over her trapped calf. The wardens' attempts to rescue the baby hippo fail when their jeep gets stuck in the mud. But if they don't free the baby soon, he and his mother will die. Can Mandy help the hippos?

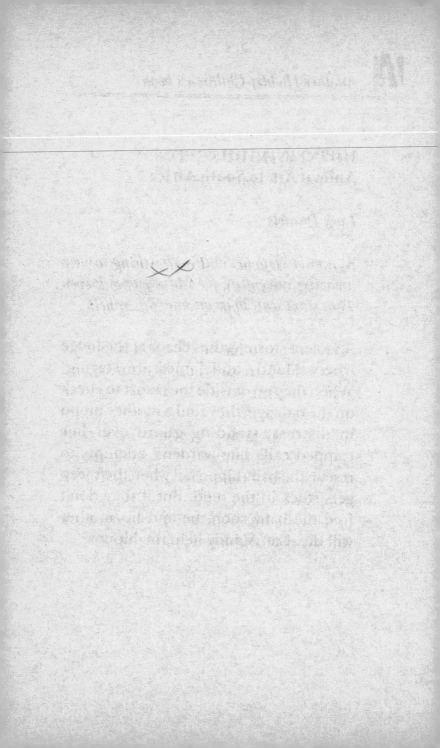

Another Hodder Children's book

DOG IN THE DUNGEON
Animal Ark Hauntings 1

Lucy Daniels

Mandy and James will do anything to help an animal in distress. And sometimes even ghostly animals appear to need their help . . .

Skelton Castle has always had a faithful deerhound to protect its family and grounds. But Aminta, the last of the line, died a short while ago. So when Mandy and James explore the creepy castle the last thing they expect to see is a deerhound – especially one which looks uncannily like Aminta . . . Could it possibly be her? And what does she want with Mandy and James?